NO

MUSIC

and other stories

JUSTIN GRIMBOL

ATLATL

Atlatl Press
POB 521
Dayton, Ohio 45401
atlatlpress.com
info@atlatlpress.com

NO

MUSIC

AND

OTHER

STORIES

Contents

NO
MUSIC

ONE

RYAN GOT OUT of the shower and walked into the kitchen. He looked out the window. The rising sun lit the trees in his backyard.

He opened a window and felt the morning breeze come in, covering his body.

Being naked felt good. He wished he could be naked more often. He wished he could jog naked. He had a great body and it deserved as much sunlight and fresh air as possible.

But that just wasn't the kind of world he lived in.

Hell, if he walked down the street naked, he'd probably only make it a few feet before Mrs. Mackonrow, his next-door neighbor, called the police.

Ryan put on his jogging shorts and the loose muscle shirt he had owned since high school, back when he was a bit of a fatty.

His dog walked up to him, its tail wagging.

"Sorry, you can't come with me, sweetie," he said.

He led the dog into the basement and put him in his crate.

Before Ryan left he got out his iPod, scrolled through to the soundtrack to *Rocky XI*, then strapped it onto his armband.

Just before putting headphones on, his phone rang. The ringer was set to sound like a rotary phone.

Ryan looked at the screen. It was his sister. He answered.

"Hey, Ryan, how you holding up?" she asked.

"I'm fine."

"Remember we have that meeting with Mom's doctor today," she said.

"Right. Thanks for reminding me."

"No problem. I'll see you then."

Wild emotions overtook him for a moment, and he hurled his phone against the wall.

It broke apart, the pieces scattering across the floor.

He could put the phone back together again. He knew that. But he decided to leave it on the floor for the time being.

Ryan walked outside and smelled the air, trying to calm himself.

He walked up to the garage and lifted the parking bay door. His bike stood in the middle of the cement floor. There was nothing else in the garage. Just the bicycle. He loved that thing.

Ryan climbed on and pedaled out in the direction of the hospital. It was ten miles away, and he knew, even if he took the long route, the one that took him past the lake for a bit, he would get to the meeting on time.

TWO

THE WAITING ROOM at the hospital was spacious. There were comfy chairs and a widescreen TV that played "family friendly" movies. Vending machines lined the walls. Windows overlooked the surrounding neighborhoods, and the lake shimmered in the distance.

Ryan's sister, Aubrey, sat with her daughter. People called the girl Snapper because she had such big teeth.

The two played with their iPads, Snapper eventually getting bored with hers and leaning against her mother's arm.

She watched her mother type emails to various family members. Snapper didn't know how to read yet, but she liked the way the letters looked. Some of the words looked big and fancy.

"Mom, can you read me what you're writing?" she asked.

"No, you don't want to hear any of this. It's boring medical stuff."

"About Grandma?"

"Yup."

The waiting room elevator's bell sounded, and the door slid open.

An overweight family stepped out.

Another elevator to the left of the first one opened. A doctor in scrubs and a loose white coat walked out, followed by Ryan, whom Snapper endearingly called Uncle Ribbon.

Snapper jumped up and ran to her uncle. He swept her up in his arms, squeezing her tight.

"Gross, you're all slimy," she said.

"Damn right, I'm slimy," he said. "It's called being in shape."

Ryan's sister looked up from her iPad and rolled her eyes, smiling.

"How's Mom?"

"Fine, I guess. I mean, she's still hooked up to all that crap, which you know she hates."

Ryan put Snapper down, kissed his sister on the forehead, and headed to his mother's room.

He walked past other sick patients with other sick smells. His mother's room was at the end of the hallway.

The machine was breathing for her. It had been like that for days. Machinery. Monitors. Tubes. Beeping. Carts stacked with medicines.

He didn't know what was wrong with her. Never really had. Something about having a congested heart. There were other things too. Lots of other things. Ryan only pretended to understand.

The doctor came in with his sister and niece to discuss the situation.

Ryan nodded as the doctor spoke, making little sighs and grunts to appear grief stricken and focused and determined, the way you are supposed to be when someone is dying.

Yet Ryan felt sexy right then. He often felt sexy when he was in the hospital. He felt sexy and proud of how in shape he was, and he always wanted to be outside with the sun warming him, riding his bike, sweating, aching.

His sister noticed his boner.

"What the fuck!" she yelped, surprised.

Snapper started laughing.

The doctor looked down and saw Ryan's cock. He managed to maintain composure.

"Do you have any questions?" he asked.

"Yeah, tons, but first I would like my brother to do something about that massive hard-on he has."

"I'm sorry," Ryan said.

"Why does it get like that?" Snapper asked.

"Are you going to explain this one?" his sister asked.

"I should get going," he said.

His sister gave him a sympathetic look and put her hand on his shoulder.

"I'm sorry for teasing you," she said.

"It's fine, really. I just need to go."

"Don't you wanna know what's going on with Mom?"

"I really need to get out of here," he said.

"Okay, I'll call you later and tell you what's going on."

Ryan's dick had grown longer. Its head stuck out the bottom of his shorts.

The doctor excused himself. He was blushing and looked dizzy.

"LOOK AT IT!" Snapper yelled.

"Shit," Ryan said.

He jogged down the corridor to the lobby. As soon as he reached the elevator, his boner had begun to shrink a bit.

At first, Ryan was embarrassed. But doctors see cocks all the time—cocks of all shapes and sizes. His sister had seen him naked tons of times when they were little. And was it even really that big of a deal for his niece to see it? If they were cave people living way back in the day, they would see each other's genitalia all the time.

It wasn't worth worrying about. Ryan just wanted to ride his bike and listen to music.

THREE

RYAN PEDALED TO the lake. He found a group of ladies sunbathing.

They liked him. They liked his body. He could tell.

He took his shirt off. He flexed his muscles.

The women snickered and giggled and started breathing heavily.

Ryan did some pushups, then flexed a little more.

He started doing some jumping jacks, which were admittedly worthless as a form of exercise, but it got his backside jiggling around. The women were cheering and laughing wildly, having a great time.

He could see them clapping their hands, could see their happiness, but he couldn't hear them. His iPod was on. The volume was as high as it could get.

Ryan started flexing again. Tightening his muscles, he howled at the summer sky.

He grabbed his shirt, got back on his bike, and rode away.

FOUR

HE WAS HALFWAY home when he realized his iPod wasn't on.

He reached for it and realized it was gone. His headphones dangled.

"Stay calm," he told himself. "Don't freak out."

Next thing Ryan knew he was on all fours, screaming and punching the cement.

His knuckles became bloodied.

His throat felt raw.

That old biddy that lived next door appeared on the front porch with a phone in her hand. It was the receiver of an old rotary phone, the cord stretched so far it looked like it was going to snap.

The sky had turned dark for him—smoky, cool, and wet.

Finally, though the panic still filled him, he was able to pull himself together. He stood and mounted his bike.

He waved to his neighbor.

She shook her head.

Ryan rode off.

FIVE

RYAN SPED BACK to the lake. He crawled on the sand, searching.

It was an expansive beach, but he was willing to comb through the entire thing, sift through each grain of sand to find the iPod.

But that was unnecessary. He soon spotted it lying in damp sand, lazy waves lapping up against it.

He scrambled over to it.

The screen was cracked.

"No," he thought. "This can't be my iPod. It can't be."

But there were his initials, engraved onto the back of the thing.

For the most part, the beach was empty.

An older gentleman walked his dog a few yards away.

About twenty feet away was a fat college-age guy with long curly hair.

"Dude," the guy said. "You are so fucking buff-looking."

Ryan looked at the fatty. He choked back tears.

"Dude, so, do you go to the gym a lot? It may not look like it, but I'm pretty buffed-out myself. I go to the gym, like, all the time. Check this out."

The fat kid got on the ground and started doing pushups.

He managed to do about five before collapsing.

Ryan sat there, not knowing what to do or say.

"Stop fuckin' looking at me!" the kid wheezed. "JUST STOP FUCKING LOOKING AT ME!"

Ryan got up and walked his bike across the sand, his broken iPod in his hand.

SIX

THAT NIGHT RYAN sat in front of the fireplace, watching the flames and thinking.

That iPod had all his songs on it. All of them.

Thousands.

Audiobooks too.

His computer had stopped working months before. So even if he had the money to buy a new iPod, he had no music to put on it.

Riding his bike and listening to music were his favorite things. At times it felt like the only thing he wanted to do—the only thing that felt like living to him.

But he couldn't imagine going on those long bike rides without music. With his iPod and sweet tunes, the bike ride became an enchanting thing. Without it, riding his bike just seemed boring.

Ryan resented how "all-or-nothing" all this new technology was. He had lost one tiny device and, with it, almost everything that filled his days with joy.

When he was in high school he had a series of Walkmans. He lost those damn things all the time, but it was no big deal. He still had his tapes and CDs. All he had to do was buy a new Walkman or borrow one from a friend. No big deal.

He missed all of that. He missed that kind of scrappy technology. It was bulky and annoying and never gave him panic attacks the way iPods and laptops did.

The next day, he decided to buy a Walkman.

He rode his bike into town. It was a boring ride. No music. Just the sound of rushing traffic.

He knew a beautiful route home that passed through a great neighborhood with charming old Danish homes with elaborate gardens. Homes that smelled like mashed potatoes and gravy.

But he didn't take that route. He rode down Route 30, past the Chinese restaurant nobody liked to go to and the gym and the Shoe Express and the Walmart.

The thrift store on Payne Avenue didn't have any Walkmans. All they had were old computer printers, alarm clocks, and early web cameras.

The place even had newer gizmos. There were Xboxes. PlayStations. First generation iPads. An iPod.

Ryan checked the price on the iPod. Seventy-eight bucks. He laughed. Even a used iPod was too expensive for him.

There was another thrift store three miles down the road, right past the abandoned, hollowed-out Blockbuster and the Pizza Shack.

It was a Goodwill. It was clean and didn't have the armpit smell the other one had.

Most importantly, he found a tape player—two, as a matter of fact—for only two bucks each.

He even bought some tapes. Some Madonna, some Billy Joel, and some classical.

This was not his kind of music, but he figured it would be a good addition to his library. And that was a good thing.

He often felt spoiled by his iPod and how he was able to download any kind of music he wanted. Technology offered too much variety.

He bought some batteries from the gas station across the street, along with an iced tea in a tall can.

The first Walkman had spiderwebs in the tape deck. This was gross, but Ryan didn't let himself get discouraged. Walkmans were durable machines, he told himself. These things were built to last.

After blowing the dust and webs out of the deck he put a tape in and pressed play.

A crackling sound came through the headphones. He liked that. It made him feel nostalgic and rustic. He was tuning into something primitive. Something strong.

Music started. There was the sound of a guitar. Then louder crackling. The guitar sound became warped and slow.

A man's voice came on. It sounded like a whale calling across deep water.

"Okay, this one must have really gone through some hell in the past dozen years," he thought.

He threw it away and tried the second one.

This one sounded better, clearer. There was still that crackling sound, but that was good. That was the sound from the past he trusted.

Billy Joel started singing.

It sounded good. It sounded pure.

He got excited.

He got onto his bike. He rode off, standing up on the pedals, bobbing his head to the music.

"I'M BACK!" he yelled.

Once he was past Nelson and heading toward the lake, he started feeling paranoid.

The song didn't have the energy he remembered it having. Had he jumped the gun?

Was this Walkman working?

He slowed down and listened carefully.

By the time he got to the beach, it was obvious the tape was playing slowly. At times the crackling was just too intense.

He tried to rewind the tape, but then the Walkman made a squealing sound and ate the analog ribbon.

Ryan lobbed the Walkman into the lake in a fury.

Some kids down the beach saw him and laughed.

He gave them a meager smile, then rode off.

SEVEN

RYAN SPENT THE next week hunting for another Walkman. He found a couple, but neither worked very well.

There was a Discman at the Salvation Army for ten bucks. It worked well, but all the CDs he bought were scratched and whenever he hit a bump in the road they would skip.

Finally, one day he took all the devices he had bought and threw them in the lake.

He thought about going for a swim, but remembered he had to get home. He had things to do.

He had to clean the gutters.

The grass in the front lawn had gotten tall and wild and he needed to mow.

And there was Charlie, his mutt. Part bull dog, part something else. He figured maybe a husky or a lab or both.

He hadn't fed him in . . . well . . . he couldn't even remember how long. At least a couple days. Maybe longer.

And Charlie had been in that crate. That goddamned crate. People swore a dog wouldn't soil their crate, that they were finicky about that sort of thing, but Ryan wasn't so sure of all that.

He pedaled home as fast as he could.

He dropped the bike off in the front yard and ran into the house.

The crate was in the basement.

It smelled bad down there.

The dog had shat in his crate. He was sure of it.

Then Ryan saw the flies.

He saw the ribs sticking out of the beast.

He puked onto the cement floor.

"Damn," he said. "Damn, damn, damn."

He opened the crate and dragged his dog's dead body out of it, up the stairs, and out into the backyard.

He dug a hole. Put the dog in it. Filled it in.

Then went back inside.

EIGHT

RYAN SPENT THE next day riding his bike with no headphones on.

He was bored. He had never felt so bored.

The sounds of traffic and sirens irritated him.

He found himself whistling Christmas carols.

Christmas was many months away.

It was time to give up. It was time to throw his bike in the lake with all the other crappy things he had bought.

He was on his way to the lake to do just that when he saw another thrift store right next to an old barbershop; the kind of barbershop that only war vets go to, with artillery in the window display. It was a den of well shaven, buzz cut wielding old men with weak chins, the adjacent thrift store an extension of the barbershop. He assumed it was run by some ornery old man, and the old man would probably take good care of his Walkmans.

Ryan went inside to take a look.

The shop was not run by an old man. The owner of this shop was a plump older woman.

Nothing was organized. Old VHS tapes were mixed together with tea cups and butt-naked Barbie dolls.

The place had lots of different stuff. It even had used dog toys. They were chewed up and mangled and stank. He found one half-chewed bone next to a DVD player.

"Can I help you?" the owner asked.

She was a gross woman. Even her eyeballs looked sweaty.

"I'm just browsing," Ryan said.

The woman scratched her crotch. It made a strange sound. Like nails on a chalkboard.

Ryan felt tense.

The woman sniffed her scratching fingers, then let out a long, satisfied sigh.

"We have lots of movies here," she said. "You like movies?"

"I'm really just browsing," Ryan said.

"Oh I know what you want," the old woman said.

She walked up to a dresser and opened one of the drawers.

For one hopeful moment Ryan thought she was going to pull out a Walkman, but instead she pulled out a stack of DVDs and brought them to him.

He looked through the stack, just trying to be polite to the sloppy old broad.

It was porn. And not just the usual naughty neighbors or ballistic blowjobs variety. It was old lady porn. Each DVD cover showed an old lady getting the steaming pink pile driver from a young stud like himself.

The owner, who was looking extra old and extra oily now, smiled at him and bit her lower lip.

He handed the DVDs back to her.

"I'm looking for a Walkman," he said.

She gave him a very grave stare.

"I have such an item," she said.

Then she led him to the back of the store. Past a pile of tampon boxes and used vinyl. Past the Tonka truck with only three wheels and the wobbly stack of VHS tapes of *Titanic*. All the way to the back of the room where a simple wooden box sat on a workbench.

The old lady opened it.

She reached in and pulled out a Walkman.

It was yellow and the casing had lettering on it saying it was waterproof and that it was made to last.

Ryan remembered those kind. The good kind. Yes, the kind that last. The kind of Walkman that was built to be durable.

He held it.

"What do you want for it?"

"For that item? For an item my own child used. An item he carried with him as he backpacked around the world, to the mountains in Alaska, where he stayed and drank and lost his mind?"

Ryan nodded.

"Three dollars," she said.

He reached into his fanny pack and pulled out a few crumpled bills. He handed them to her.

A gentle rain was coming down outside as Ryan left the store.

He worried for a moment, trying to shield the Walkman from the rain, but then remembered its waterproof guarantee.

He pressed play.

He could hear things moving in the device. He could hear sounds coming from the headphones. It was working. It already had batteries.

He put the headphones on.

He could hear music.

The headphones weren't earbuds. They were the old round kind, the kind covered with soft foam.

They felt so soft.

And the music was so engrossing.

He loved it.

He didn't recognize the band but he loved their sound. The way they incorporated the saxophone and the keyboard, and there was something else, something that sounded like a whale singing.

Ryan got on his bike and rode off.

He rode out of town, up Mount Willoupy, and then down.

He rode fast. As he sped downhill, he didn't once use his brakes.

Ryan cursed and screamed and laughed and made hyena sounds. Sounds of pure joy and relief.

NINE

RYAN BECAME OBSESSED with the Walkman and the tape left in it, which he assumed had belonged to the old lady's son.

He went bike riding every day, often for ten or twelve hours at a time.

When he wasn't riding he was at the lake doing pushups for the ladies.

Months passed, and fall came. The leaves turned the color of street lamps. There were not as many twenty-year-old women at the beach to show his body off to, so he started going to yoga.

The women in yoga loved him. He was big but flexible.

He caught women staring at the strip of sweat that ran down the back of his running shorts.

They looked horny.

Ryan had a job. That was the only reason he didn't ride his bike all day long. He worked as a trainer at Twenty-Four-Hour Fitness. He often worked his clients so hard they would pass out, and he would have to sneak them into the locker room when the boss wasn't looking and smack them around to revive them. When they came to he would threaten them.

"If you complain, I will hunt your dweeby ass down," he would say.

Ryan himself did not enjoy the gym. Not anymore, anyway. It was too modern. Too many gizmos. Everything was electric. The elliptical. The stair climbers. The rowing machines. It was all too fancy. There was even a television screen that played Rocky movies, but never the old ones. Just the newer installments. *Rocky XX*, where he becomes an exorcist. *Rocky XXV*, where he goes back to high school and gets really into dry humping. Ryan didn't like those movies anymore. There was too much CGI. He couldn't stand crap like that.

Ryan's Walkman had helped him embrace the more rustic side of life. Instead of lifting weights he would ride his bike up mountains, hike into the woods, find big rocks and throw them around. He chopped wood, more than he would ever need. His backyard was filled with large stacks of dry logs. And he rode. He rode his bike long and hard and fast. He would off-road and ride his bike through shallow sections of creeks, through raging rapids.

Once he fell off and was worried the Walkman had broken, but it hadn't. It was waterproof.

The music was just so intense, so empowering, so engrossing to his soul. It made him want to constantly push himself to the limits.

Ryan got big. Really big.

He rode around town in the snowy months of January and February, topless, the snowflakes melting as they landed on his warm muscles.

He ran into a friend of his sister's at the grocery store. She told him he looked gross and that his muscles were too big.

Ryan knew this was true. He knew he had grown so musclebound things had become freakish and unflattering.

Still, he was proud of what he was.

He felt durable.

He became too manly for yoga.

The flexing helped him tone his muscles, but he didn't like how calm and peaceful everyone acted. Ryan preferred to feel more savage than that.

The yoga instructor didn't like that he wore his headphones during class. She felt it was disrespectful and awkward.

One day, during yoga, he started moaning and growling and humming along to the music playing on the Walkman.

The people in the class became agitated and upset. They packed their mats and left.

The instructor asked Ryan not to come back.

He was fine with that.

He was tired of yoga.

He was tired of women. Normal women, at least.

He longed to seduce a wilder creature. Not these uptight yuppies, squeezing a bit of exercise into their day.

Ryan needed his libido to be tested. To be pushed to the edge of savagery.

TEN

ONE NIGHT, RYAN got so horny he became delirious.

He tried calming himself with pushups but he could feel his pecker head butting up against the floor.

There was a biker bar at the end of town. Ryan ventured in, hoping to find a tougher sort of lady.

He sat at a booth and ordered a whiskey.

There weren't many people there. Just a few old tattooed men and the bartender, who was old. Really old. She moved slow. It took her a while to get Ryan's drink.

"Can you move that old ass?" he said. "I'm rotting away over here!"

The old men didn't like his attitude.

"You need to watch your mouth!" one of them said.

Ryan blew the old man a kiss.

The old man got up, laced his fingers, and bent them outwards against each other until they cracked.

Ryan took his shirt off.

He spit on his hand and rubbed it on his huge pectoral muscles.

"You want some of this, old man?" he said.

The old man lunged at him.

A fight broke out.

Ryan kept his headphones on and listened to his sweet tunes as he brutalized the old bikers.

ELEVEN

THE LAST THING Ryan could remember was stomping an old man, then going behind the bar and upending a bottle of whiskey like it was Gatorade.

He remembered moaning sounds.

He remembered picking a tooth out of his knuckles.

When he came to, his dick was deep in the anus of a black bear. He was giving it long strokes.

The bear moaned. Ryan had its arms pinned down. The beast's ear had been ripped off. It hung from Ryan's mouth.

Ryan spat it out and laughed.

How the fuck did I get here? he wondered.

He saw his Walkman on the ground. He picked it up. Put the headphones on.

The music sounded even louder, even more rocking than usual.

Ryan humped to the beat.

His dick felt impossibly hard.

After he fucked the bear he punched it in the head a bunch of times until it was sleeping. He let it nap there and then he walked down the mountain, found a creek, and bathed in the icy water.

He was lost. But he didn't mind.

He jogged around the forest listening to his Walkman, feeling the way he imagined men—real men—used to feel back in the day. Back when there was no such thing as online dating and supermarkets and all that nonsense.

There were no traffic sounds in these woods. Hours passed, and Ryan never even saw a plane fly overhead.

TWELVE

SNAPPER WAS AT a birthday party at the lake. This was the first birthday party she had been invited to in a long time, and she was really excited.

Her friend Cassidy was turning seven.

Snapper had bought her friend a dog collar that glowed in the dark and played music.

Cassidy didn't own a dog. The other kids saw the present and laughed.

Snapper felt so embarrassed she had to fight to hold back tears.

Cassidy was a tall girl, a confident girl, and she had a good sense of humor. She told Snapper to stop crying. Then Cassidy put the collar on herself and started making barking sounds until the music turned on and then all the girls started dancing around and laughing.

They stayed at the lake all day and played Marco Polo and queen of the raft.

Snapper was the runt of the group and kept getting knocked off the raft and falling into the water.

There were moments when Snapper wanted to bite the raft or at least some of the legs that were dangling off it.

But she remembered what her grandmother said. Her grandmother always told her if she felt the need to bite, to laugh instead.
"And if laughing doesn't help, then make animal noises. Never be
ashamed of feeling a little like a beast," her grandmother had said.
"We all have that in us."

So, while everyone else hung out on the big blow-up raft, Snapper started making weird noises. Really strange noises.

The other kids were annoyed by this. All but Cassidy. She
thought it was funny.

She jumped off the raft and joined Snapper in the cool water.

"What are you doing?" Cassidy said.

"Making shark noises," Snapper said.

Cassidy liked that. She laughed and hugged her tiny friend.

Cassidy and Snapper decided they didn't want to be queens of
the raft; they wanted to be queens of the lake. They controlled the
waves, and splashed all the girls on the raft.

For dinner, Cassidy's father brought pizza.

Snapper ate three slices. Cassidy was impressed.

Afterwards the kids sang the birthday song as the adults
brought out ice cream cake.

As she dug her plastic fork into the cake, Snapper saw a man
emerging from the woods out of the corner of her eye.

The other girls noticed the creepy man as well. They remarked
that he was homeless and that he was always listening to a Walkman. They said he stank and said gross things.

Snapper thought the man looked happy. He was dancing and
exercising and had lots of cool-looking muscles.

She snuck away from the grownups to talk to the man.

It wasn't until she got close that she realized he was her uncle.

"UNCLE RIBBON!" she screamed.

She ran up to the guy.

Ryan looked confused at first, but then started laughing. He picked Snapper up and tickled her.

"I haven't seen you in a really long time," Snapper said. "Where have you been?"

Ryan didn't respond. He just smiled at his sweet niece and licked his thumb and used it to wipe off the ice cream gathered at the edge of Snapper's mouth.

"What's that?" she asked.

She pointed at his Walkman.

Her uncle looked excited.

He put the headphones over her ears and pressed play.

"It doesn't work," she said.

His eyes became wide and his expression unnerving.

"All it does is make a crackling sound," she said.

"IT WORKS JUST FINE!" Ryan insisted, taking the headphones back.

He put them on and pressed play.

"What did you do to it?" he screamed. "You broke it!"

"I didn't do anything," Snapper insisted.

Ryan grabbed her. He picked her up and looked into her scared little girl eyes.

"YOU BROKE IT!" he yelled.

He lifted Snapper over his head. She was screaming now, and grownups were looking over at them.

Ryan took a few steps toward the beach and hurled Snapper into the lake.

He threw her far out into the water.

She made a huge splash.

Cassidy's dad ran across the beach and dove into the water.

The other men were inching toward Ryan.

They were nervous but protective of the stunned children.

Ryan fumbled with the Walkman desperately. For the first time since buying it, he opened the tape deck.

It was empty.

Ryan looked at all the men, tears streaming down his face.

"It's not working," he said.

THIRTEEN

RYAN HAD THE jail cell to himself. He liked it that way.

The guard was Sammy Rogan, an old classmate from high school.

Ryan's Walkman had been confiscated. He had tried to explain to Sammy how it played music even though there was no tape and, as it turned out, no battery.

"It's fucking really epic shit too," Ryan said. "You really should find it and listen to it."

Sammy smiled at him through thin lips.

FOURTEEN

RYAN SLEPT WELL in his cell.

He slept all night and through the next day, and when he woke he felt replenished but still sleepy. After eating a cheese sandwich brought to him by the guard, he slept some more.

He dreamed of the lake and the waves.

A fleet of owls flew overhead. Beyond the owls a gray sky filtered the sun.

Ryan woke up to the sound of keys turning.

He opened his eyes to three old women entering his cell.

They were very old and very naked.

At first he didn't recognize them.

One was the old lady from the thrift shop who had sold him the Walkman. Another was his mother.

He had a boner. A big one. The old women took note and shook their heads.

"I'm sorry," he kept saying. "I can't help it."

GRANDMAFACE

YOUR SUNDAY BEST

"GET THE FUCK OUT OF HERE!" Wendy yelled. "YOU'RE NOT WELCOME HERE, FUCKFACE!"

The postal worker slid the mail into the mailbox and ran back to his van.

"YOU PERVERT! THAT MAIL BETTER NOT SMELL LIKE YOUR DICK! I KNOW WHAT YOUR DICK SMELLS LIKE, MOTHERFUCKER! YOU CAN'T FOOL ME WITH YOUR MAILMAN BULLSHIT, MOTHERFUCKER!"

Wendy's dog, Murphy, sat behind her, shaking.

"Come on, Murphy!" she said. "Bark at him. You're a dog. Go bark. Act crazy."

The dog whimpered. He was acting pitiful. So Wendy started howling at the sun. Murphy couldn't help but join in. Soon they were both howling and it sounded beautiful to both of them and Murphy was now in a much better mood.

SUNDAY SCHOOL

ONCE THE MAILMAN was gone, Wendy walked out across the front yard and pulled two letters out of the mailbox. She looked them over. One letter was from her mother. The card showed a picture of a big woman and daughter riding a Harley together, looking cool in a goofy way. Above the picture were the words HAPPY MOTHER'S DAY.

She opened the card. Her mother had shaky handwriting.

Just wanted to say happy Mother's Day to my favorite daughter, it read.

Wendy's mother didn't understand how this holiday worked. She needed to call her mom, to set things straight.

The phone rang a few times. She heard the woman clear her voice and say hello.

"Hey, Mom, happy Mother's Day," Wendy said.

"Happy Mother's Day to you."

"No, Mom, that's not how it works. I'm the one who is supposed to celebrate you. You don't have to send me cards and crap like that. I'm the one who is supposed to be sending you cards."

"Did you?"

"Did I what?"

"Did you send me a card?"

"No."

"So what's the problem? Wendy, honey, can't we just be nice to each other?"

Wendy groaned.

"So how else are things?" her mom asked. "How are you?"

"Oversexed."

"Oh stop."

"Can't stop. Won't stop."

"Hey, can I ask you something?" Wendy's mother asked.

"What?"

"Have you gone to the salon lately?"

"Nope."

"It's just I've been hearing rumors around town that your hair is looking extra shaggy recently."

"Rumors? Really?"

"You have such a pretty face, with those high cheek bones and those smiley eyes. I just don't see why you don't take care of your hair."

"Mom, my hair looks messy no matter what I do with it."

"Now, that's not true. I took you to that Carol's Salon and she did a great job on your hair."

"Last time I went to her she made me look like a GI Joe."

"She cut it short."

"I hated it. I hate the barber. I hate the salon. It's in her gross basement."

There was a long silence.

"Are you going to come over today?" her mother asked.

"Sure, Mom."

"How 'bout you come over for dinner?"

"What are you having?"

"I planned on getting pizza. Your favorite."

"I'm on a diet."

"You are not."

"Am too."

She got off the phone.

She cuddled with her dog on the couch for a while.

Then she called the pizza place and ordered a large pie of pizza with extra cheese.

CHURCH

TWO ELDERLY DOGS wandered into Wendy's backyard. They looked old and haggard. She tried to pet the dogs, but they growled at her. After that, Wendy took to watching from a distance. Even though they came every few days, they treated her like a stranger. They never seemed to remember her or all the treats she had left for them. She figured most likely they suffered from doggy Alzheimer's or some other form of dementia.

On this day, as they usually did, the old dogs started humping each other. Wendy was glad they felt comfortable doing this. She was proud her poorly kept backyard ignited passion in these elderly dogs.

Murphy came out to the back porch to sit by Wendy and watched the other dogs hump.

"Go on, Murph," she said. "Get in there."

Her dog looked up at her, shaking his tail. He nudged Wendy's leg with his smooth amber-colored forehead. His eyes looked so pitiful. Wendy leaned down and kissed his snout.

They sat there together and watched the stray dogs hump.

PRAY AND STUFF

THE PHONE RANG. Wendy answered and belched hello.

Her father was on the other line.

"How's my little girl?" he asked.

"Doing good, Dad."

"How's that thing you hang out in? The box-like thing? With the stuff?"

"My house. It's great."

"That's great. I'm glad."

"When are you coming to visit me?"

"Never, probably."

"What if I made that beef stew you like so much?"

"Dieting."

"What do you eat now, Dad?"

"Grass mainly. I'm a farmer."

"That's awesome. Can I come live on the farm?"

"No, you're way too spoiled. That's actually why I am calling. To apologize for spoiling you so hard."

"Dad, I'm so sick of you apologizing about that."

"Well . . ."

"Dad, you should come visit and play Ring and Run with me."

"I'm sure you can play it by yourself."

"Well yeah, obviously, but you were always so much fun."

"I am really fun. The other farmers love me. They say I am really good at eating grass. Best they've seen. And the women out here are really impressive."

"How so?"

"Curvy. Lots of warmth."

"Everything's warm."

"Not everything."

"Dad, stop being a fucking jerk. Come home. I love you."

"I also drink lots of milk here. Right out of the cow's titty. Your mother never let me have a cow. Your mother hated cows. I think she was jealous of their titties."

"Dad, she just got bored of talking about them so much."

"That's the problem with you women. You don't appreciate boredom. People here love it. They fucking love it. They love it so fucking much."

"I'm actually pretty mature now. I like to get boring. I walk my dog a lot."

"That's the wrong kind of boring."

"Whatever you say, Dad."

"So you are doing okay?"

"No, 'cause you're being a fucking prick."

"I have a lot of work to do, honey."

"I'm going to sue you."

"I'm sure."

"What if you eat too much grass?"

"No such thing."

"What if I become president and make farming illegal?"

"I would still keep on farming. I'm very loyal to the trade."

"Okay, Dad. I have to go now."

"You okay financially?"

"I'm fine."
"Okay."
She hung up the phone.

HYMNS

HEAT LIGHTNING FLASHED in the distance. Wendy sat on her friend Rebecca's back porch, gazing out over the shadows of the mountains.

"We should wear polo shirts," Wendy said. "That way we would look more professional. I'm tired of looking so unprofessional."

"I don't know about that. I'd probably just look like a soccer mom."

"Soccer's amazing!" Wendy said.

"My kid doesn't play sports. He plays spin the bottle. He plays that fucking game all the time."

"I know. I saw his chapped lips."

"He and all his friends have these horrible little monster mouths. The girls do too."

"Maybe that's what's popular," Wendy said, tracing her finger across a weathered floorboard.

"Who knows? When we were young we played those awkward sex games too. But we at least brought chapstick with us."

"Because we were responsible," Wendy said, smirking.

"Yes," Rebecca said. "If I had one word to describe our

adolescence, I would say it was responsible."

They laughed.

Fireflies hovered over the field, their butts glowing for a moment before fading and coming back to life.

"I should move in here," Wendy said. "I like this place."

"You have your own house that your mom pays for."

"Come on. Think of the good times we could have. We could wear polo shirts and eat pizza. I have been eating a lot of pizza lately."

"Listen," Rebecca said, "if you lived with me, my poor son would never stop jerking off. I don't think he could handle his puberty getting any more out of control."

"He has a little crush on me," Wendy admitted.

"He especially likes you now that you eat all that pizza. It's exciting for a fatty like him to see a skinny lady eat like that. A couple nights ago he saw you in the pizza place. He said you took down a whole pie and that you looked so out of it you didn't even recognize him."

"That might have happened," Wendy said.

"He couldn't understand why you aren't fat yet. I had to give him a little talk about what a metabolism is. It got awkward. It was worse than the sex talk."

"I just really want to live here and I don't like you changing the subject like this," Wendy said.

"Wendy, he went through my photo album. And took out a picture of you."

"Which one?"

"The one where we switched bathing suits."

Wendy remembered that photo well. She had a framed copy of it in her house. Rebecca and she had switched bathing suits one day at the lake. Rebecca was tall and hefty. Wendy was also tall but scrawny and muscular. Their bathing suits didn't fit each other well. Rebecca's one-piece was too big for Wendy and looked more like a pair of overalls. Her breasts lay bare in the shot.

"I'm flattered."

"I figured you would be."

"But isn't it kinda weird?" Wendy said. "I mean, you're in the picture too. My bikini was so small on you it was like you had four boobs."

"It wasn't my best moment."

"So if your kid has that picture and is jerking his little wiener to it, then that means he's not just looking at me. He's looking at you. At least a little."

"Fuck, I hadn't thought of that before."

"It's either messed up or your kid is just really sophisticated sexually."

"Oh come on."

"You should punish him. You should spank him."

"You know," Rebecca said, "I never understood all the weird mean ways our mothers punished us. You know, all the spanking and stuff like that. But right now, when I think about that picture and his scabby lips, I just want to shove soap in his mouth."

"That would be hilarious. You should do it."

"I'm pretty sure that would be abuse."

"No, it's more like a prank."

"What's the worst thing your parents ever did to you?" Rebecca asked.

"Just being in my life, for the most part. Calling me. Talking to me. It can get pretty terrible."

"No, I mean as punishment."

"Oh, right," Wendy said. "They weren't into physical punishment. They didn't spank me or anything. Which was good 'cause I always thought spanking was awkward. 'Cause it's sexual, you know? It's something people do when they are being kinky."

"I spanked my kid once. I felt awful about it."

"What happened?" Wendy said.

47

"It was after the divorce. Well, not right after it. Like, two years later. Anyway, Tim had found all the old pictures, all the old family pictures I had put in the basement because I didn't want to look at them anymore. He put them up around the house."

"That's just sad though," Wendy said, frowning. "It's not really that bad of a thing."

"I know. But it freaked me out. I yelled at him. And he told me to shut the fuck up and that's when I lost it."

"You spanked him?"

"I did. Not hard, but still . . . I spanked my kid. I had always promised myself I would never do that."

"But you did. You big jerk. You spanked your kid. Right on the butt. No wonder he stole that picture. He's confused."

"Oh shut up."

"I got spanked once. Not by my parents though."

"I'm sure you've gotten spanked by half this town," Rebecca remarked.

"No, I'm not talking about fun spanking. I mean, I got spanked as a punishment. When I was little. Like a little kid. Well, not that little. I was a teenager. Well, sorta. I was twelve."

"Who spanked you?"

"You remember Grandmaface?"

"Sure, he had that wrinkly face when he was young."

"He's still wrinkly. Anyway. For a while, he used to live with his uncle who was this creepy born-again dude. And one day we stole these big crosses he had in his living room. We played swords with them. He got mad. Spanked us."

"Both of you?"

Wendy nodded while lighting a cigarette.

"Both of us. He really went to town, too," Wendy said.

"It only happened once?"

"No, it happened a second time. I tried to get him back for the spanking by peeing in his shampoo."

"He caught you peeing in his shampoo?"

"No," Wendy said, exhaling smoke. She turned to Rebecca. "For some reason nobody ever catches me doing that."

"Then what did he catch you doing?"

"I think he caught us playing with crosses again."

"What a creepy fucker."

"He wasn't so bad," Wendy said. "Just a little out of whack."

"It's not okay to spank other people's kids."

"I don't think it's normal to spank your own kids," Wendy said. "But people do it. You did it."

"Because I didn't know what else to do. I wanted to cry and break things. Spanking the little brat seemed like a better option."

"But he wasn't being a brat. He was just putting up old photos."

"Of his shitty father," Rebecca said.

"Still, you spanked his butt. You touched his butt with your hand."

"Are you really trying to compare me to that creep right now? What do you know, Wendy? You don't have kids. It fucks with your head."

"You're the one that's being judgmental. I'm just saying what that guy did wasn't that bad."

BAPTISM

THE COUCH WAS long and comfortable and smelled old. Not dusty or moldy. Just old. Wendy loved sleeping at Rebecca's place. Rebecca had inherited lots of nice things like the old couch and the grandfather clock and the old piano. Wendy felt like she could nap in that old home all day. But as soon as she heard her friend moving around the kitchen, she got up, not able to shake the feeling that she would miss something if she continued sleeping.

"Where are you going?"

"It's Sunday. I'm a minister. I have to go to work."

"I wanna go with."

"No, go back to sleep. We had a long night."

"I wanna go."

"But I don't want you to go."

"Why not?"

"Just respect my boundaries here, okay? I love you. I just don't want you to see me preach. I need you to be okay with that."

"You used to take me to church all the time. I saw you preach at First Presbyterian lots of times."

"This new place is different," Rebecca said.

"I really, really want to go."

"Just, please, drop it."

Rebecca got up and walked over to Wendy, who was still warm from sleep. Rebecca kissed her on the arms and cheeks and eyelids. She kissed her on her mouth. Wendy bit Rebecca's lower lip gently and tugged on it.

"Do you have any microwave pizza here?" Wendy asked, stretching.

"No. But you can order some Gino's if you want. They deliver."

"I haven't had Gino's in a while. Thanks."

Rebecca walked out the door and to her truck.

Wendy managed to go back to sleep for a bit. She woke up at ten and tried to order some pizza. Gino's was closed. Wendy annoyed until she remembered that most people didn't order pizza so early in the morning.

Tim came downstairs and poured a massive bowl of cereal. He sat next to Wendy.

"Why aren't you at church?" she asked.

"Mom won't let me go. Says I'm too young."

"That's strange."

"I think it's good. I don't want to go to church. You ever been to church? It's so boring."

"It's usually really fucking boring, that's true. But don't you want to see your mom preach? I've heard she's wild."

"No, I don't."

Wendy got herself a bowl of cereal. It was a poor substitute for pizza. She really wanted pizza. She told herself that on the way home she was going to stop for pizza.

"When is your mom going to be home?"

"She won't be home until night."

"Seriously?"

"Yeah. She hikes afterwards. She says it helps her heal from

51

the service."

"What the hell are her sermons like? I'm so fucking curious."

"I'm not."

Wendy looked at Tim. "You dating anyone yet?"

He shook his head no.

"You making out, though?"

"Sometimes."

"Is that why your lips are all chapped?"

"I hold the record for longest make-out. I went two hours straight."

"What's the furthest you ever went with a girl?"

Tim shrugged. "Making out."

"You made out for two hours straight and you didn't cop a cheapy?"

"Everyone was watching."

"Dude. Have you ever seen tits or a butt or anything?"

"On the internet."

"It's different in real life."

"How? Do they edit them on the internet? Those porns seem pretty low budget. I can't imagine they use many special effects to change bodies."

"They don't. At least I don't think. That's not what I mean. But when you see a butt in person, it's different. Trust me."

"I guess."

"You wanna see my butt?"

He laughed nervously.

"I'm serious. I'll show you my butt. For research. But you can't tell your mom, okay?"

He nodded.

She stood up and moved her hips in a seductive manner. She lowered her underpants and bent over a bit. She turned her head and saw how overwhelmed he was.

"Remember to breathe," she said.

He nodded.

"It doesn't look that different, right? You can see some peach fuzz and some blemishes but, otherwise, not that different. Now, watch this."

She quickly spread her ass apart, stretching it as far as it could go.

"Holy fuck!" Tim yelled.

She laughed, trying to spread it even wider.

At first Tim felt completely overwhelmed but as she kept it open for him he began to study it. Around the anus the skin looked darker and rougher. There were some hairs. They weren't big and coarse, but they were too long to be considered peach fuzz. He liked that inner region. He liked the rough skin and the purplish tint it had. The freckle near her anus. And he loved the anus itself. It looked glossy and mangled. She was able to make it open a little and shut like the hungry mouth of a baby bird. He laughed, but only to be polite. In reality he thought it was beautiful.

He thought it was heartbreaking.

Tim got closer to it. There was a strange odor. He couldn't place it, though it wasn't feces. Not really.

It was the most human thing he had ever smelled.

After about ten minutes she became tired and stopped.

She pulled up her underpants and made him promise not to tell anyone.

"I'm serious. Don't be a little tattle-tale. I'll fist fight you."

"I promise," he said.

"If I find out you bragged to your friends about seeing my but-thole, I will punch you in the mouth so many times. I swear to fucking Christ."

"I promise I won't."

"I should get going."

"Maybe you can show me your butt one more time."

"I really need to get going."

Wendy put her pants on and patted Tim on the head. She said goodbye and walked out into the humid summer day.

On her way home Wendy became increasingly anxious. She realized she had never left Murphy alone for this long. She sped down the road in her Saab, moving down the twisting country roads at a dangerous speed.

When she finally got into town, she ran two red lights. Luckily no police patrol cars saw her. She made it home without being pulled over.

COMMUNION

GRANDMAFACE AND WENDY went to the Headlights Bar and Grill on the outskirts of town. They ordered a pitcher of Miller Lite. It came with two plastic cups.

"I should have brought my dog," Wendy said.

"This place doesn't allow dogs," Grandmaface said.

"That's true. Still, I feel bad. The thing's so lonely. It has no doggy friends. It needs doggy friends."

"I know a dog that Murphy could be friends with," Grandmaface said. "It's this old mutt. I think it's blind. Maybe a little mentally ill. He looked lonely. I figured your dog needs a friend."

"My dog's young and sprightly, though."

"But he has no friends. This old dog could be a friend."

"I guess we can set them up. Is this old dog a stray?"

"No. It belongs to the old guy that works at a bar in Loaf. Ray Sanborn."

"Is this some warped, wrinkly-faced way of flirting with me?"

Grandmaface shook his head, laughed, and drank the rest of his beer in a single, intimidating gulp.

THE DINER

WENDY WALKED HER dog around Burtonsville. It was a small town. Downtown had a creek and a diner and a fire station. And that was it. She lived toward the edge of town. They walked a couple miles before letting the dog swim in the creek. Then she brought Murphy into the diner and ordered them both a milkshake.

"I found you a friend," she told her dog. "We're going to meet him tomorrow. I want you to try and be nice to him."

Her dog looked happy. Maybe he didn't need friends.

She drank her milkshake until she got a brainfreeze.

"DEAR FUCKING GOD, HAVE FUCKING MERCY!"

Some old men laughed. She looked over at them and growled. Then her dog started growling too.

MINISTERS

"IS IT ALIVE?" Wendy asked.

She knew, for the most part, that it was alive. It was sitting up and breathing. Other than that, the Newfoundland looked like something from the beyond. Its eyes were white as a shark's belly and surrounded by all sorts of crust. Its lower jaw looked like it was going to fall off. There were bandages on his arms and legs, splotches of yellow mottling the cotton wraps. His hind legs rested on a slab of wood with wheels on the bottom, one of the wheels missing. A colostomy bag rested to the side of it. That didn't look like it worked correctly either.

"He's a good boy," his owner, Ray, said.

Ray looked to be a man of leisure, which Wendy respected, though the sweat suit and Ugg boots threw her off a bit. He offered her a Hot Pocket and she refused.

Grandmaface and Ray sat on a long, worn couch and ate their Hot Pockets, insisting Wendy sit as well. She declined, feeling anxious.

"His name's Magnus," Ray said, gesturing with the Hot Pocket toward the old dog.

"Great name," Grandmaface said.

Murphy kept close to Wendy for a bit, his apprehension visible. After some time, slowly, he crept up to Magnus. He sniffed the old dog. At first Magnus didn't seem to notice Murphy. Then the decaying beast turned its head slowly and licked Murphy's face.

Wendy sighed. She felt as if she might cry. She had no idea how nice it would be to see Murphy get along with another animal.

She wanted to jump around, maybe do some jump-kicks. She held back. If she started acting out, Murphy would get distracted and want to play with her. She wanted Murphy and the decrepit hound to bond.

ASH WEDNESDAY

THE TWO DOGS, their owners, and Grandmaface reconvened the following afternoon. Ray suggested they take the dogs for a walk. Wendy couldn't imagine Magnus walking until Ray pointed to the dog's favorite wheelbarrow.

Grandmaface loaded the dog into the wheelbarrow and they headed down the street.

The evening light was fading, and the air felt like it was beginning to cool.

The fivesome walked to Mashed Potato Park. Grandmaface dumped the big Newfoundland out of the wheelbarrow. It lay in the shaded grass, breathing slowly.

At first Murphy rested with his new dog friend but quickly grew bored. Wendy could tell how restless the younger animal was. She became nervous, wanting this new friendship to be good and satisfying.

Murphy was determined to make the situation fun. As he let his new friend rest he would sprint away, then come barreling back and leap over the mountainous old Newfoundland. He used the fellow dog like a hurdle, seemingly never growing tired of his own game.

Wendy cheered him on.

"Thanks for doing this," she said to Grandmaface.

"No problem. Dogs need friends."

"What are you doing tonight? We should celebrate by eating pizza and drinking beers."

"I have dinner plans. With a woman."

"No shit! Who?"

"She's younger. You wouldn't know her."

"Oh dear god, how much younger?"

"Relax. She's not, like, twelve. She's out of diapers."

"Well that's good."

"She is young though. Nineteen. Looks even younger."

"Like me?"

"Even younger looking than you."

"You're saying I look old?"

He laughed and shook his head.

"She still has braces."

"Oh fuck."

"She's a confusing girl. I don't know why she wants to find this fucked up wrinkly face between her legs. Usually older women like me. Younger women are supposed to be vain."

"Hey, it's not like teenage boys are much better," Wendy said. "It's not like she has a choice between you or some pimply scrawny twerp. Most teenage boys look awkward, just in a smoother way."

"Were you attracted to any of the boys you dated in high school?"

"Yeah. This one guy had me so turned on I had to wear adult-sized diapers just to deal with the moisture."

"Who was he?"

"This guy I dated at camp. He was super fat. I was thirteen. He was sixteen. I would climb all over him. Like he was a jungle gym."

"Did you really wear diapers?"

"No."

"Don't be embarrassed," Grandmaface said. "I think it's an okay thing to do."

She smiled and leaned her head on his shoulder.

"No," she said. "As fun as it seems, I don't wear diapers."

PEWS

THE WATER AT the creek was too high and rough. Wendy wanted to take her dog swimming but she didn't want him swept away by the current then mangled by jagged rocks. So she took him to Lake Chaplin. The park did not allow dogs, but Wendy snuck him in anyway. The lifeguards were teenaged and looked like they were about to pass out. Even if they had noticed Murphy, they most likely wouldn't have said much.

They swam together for a bit, roughhousing in the cool water. Wendy lifted the mutt above her head and slammed him down into the water over and over again until he was exhausted and stumbled to a shady tree to take a nap.

Wendy swam laps. When she swam she went as deep as she could go, skimming the bottom with her chest and belly, rarely coming up for air.

After a while she stood up to catch her breath for a bit. As she wiped the beads of water from her face, she spied Rebecca standing waist deep in the water a few yards away. Wendy's instinct was to sneak away. Tim was a blabbermouth and had more than likely told his mother about seeing Wendy's butthole. She fought the instinct to flee, however. She was enjoying the lake, and her dog looked so peaceful in the shade of the tree. In fact, she felt a pang of homesickness for her friend and suddenly wanted very much to be near her. Wendy slid beneath the water again, maneuvering across the bottom like a fish. She came upon Rebecca and bit her gently on the ass. Wendy stood up into the sun, sputtering water and laughing. Rebecca smiled at her.

"I knew it was you," she said.

"Really? I thought I was being so sneaky."

Rebecca hugged Wendy, holding her close. She kissed her damp hair.

"Where's Murphy? I miss that dog."

"He's napping over there." Wendy shrugged her shoulder in the direction of the tree. "He made a friend recently. A dog friend. Friendship is tiring, though. He takes a lot of naps now."

"I'm so glad. What kinda dog?"

"It's an older gentleman."

"What do you mean?" Rebecca asked.

"It's just old. That's all."

"How old?"

"It looks like it's seen both world wars."

Rebecca laughed and splashed her friend.

"Seriously. I don't even know if the thing is alive, but at least Murphy has a friend."

"That's good."

Wendy gave her friend a devilish smile, then charged her and climbed onto her shoulders, pitching them both into the lake. They wrestled for a bit in the warm, shallow water. Wendy pulled the strap of Rebecca's swimsuit down, Rebecca's boob flopping out of the fabric. Rebecca quickly covered her breast with one arm and pushed Wendy with the other.

"My son is here with his friends. I don't want them to see my boob."

"What's the big deal? It's just a boob. A really big one. Really

63

big. I mean, it's an impossibly big boob."

"I'm fucking serious." Rebecca pulled the strap back onto her shoulder.

"Fine, I'm sorry. Relax."

The two women stood silently for a moment.

"I'm so worn out," Rebecca said.

"Why?"

"Church. My sermons really kick my ass. I'm usually emotionally hungover and my muscles ache."

"Fuck, what are these sermons like?"

Rebecca ignored the question.

Tim swam up to them from the shore. Wendy felt anxious and shy in the boy's presence.

"Hey, Wendy," Tim said. "I saw Murphy here. He's so cute."

Wendy nodded, looking down at her feet through the water. She dug her toes into the mucky bottom.

"Mom, my friends and I were wondering if we could go walk that trail around the woods."

"Of course," she said. "But, Tim, if I smell cigarette smoke on you I am going to be livid. I mean it. I am going to freak out in front of everyone. I am going to yell at you so loudly, most likely someone is going to call child protective services and take you away."

Tim laughed and hugged his mom.

"No cigarettes, I promise. There is always a chance an orgy might break out though. Just a heads up."

"Heaven help us all!" Rebecca sighed.

"Don't worry. It won't be full penetration. Just a little kissing and dry humping."

"But sweetie your little mouth just healed. You looked like a hideous, deformed monster for a while there." Rebecca took Tim's chin in her hand, playfully waggling his head from side to side.

"Thanks, Mom," he said, pulling away. "That's so good for my self-esteem."

Wendy tried to laugh but all she could muster was an awkward imitation of a chuckle.

She couldn't believe how casual Tim was acting. He was so comfortable around her. Maybe he had blocked the memory of her butthole from his mind. Or maybe her butthole just wasn't that big of a deal. Maybe this had happened to him before. Wendy felt a mixture of sour emotions. She wanted to swim to the bottom of the lake and lie there and scream for a really long time.

Finally Tim swam away and joined his friends. Wendy calmed a bit.

"Do you really think they are going to dry hump each other?" Wendy asked.

"I really hope not."

"You should let him go to church with you."

"What do you mean?"

"The kid seems spiritually confused."

"He's fine. He's a teenage boy. A bit horny. A bit too comfortable talking about sex with his mother. But otherwise fine."

"I don't know. He seems needy. I just think church would help."

"When did you become such an advocate for church?"

"I'm not."

Wendy and Rebecca floated on their backs for a while. The water muffled and blocked the sounds of the dry world. Wendy drifted quietly, bumping into Rebecca's arm with her head. She reached over and tickled her friend's belly.

Rebecca laughed and the two began to wrestle again. This time things got intense. The teenage lifeguard blew her whistle. She told the women to stop roughhousing or leave the park.

They apologized.

Wendy looked over to check on Murphy.

"Fuck!" she yelled.

"What's going on?" Rebecca asked.

"My fucking dog's gone. God fucking damn it!"

"He'll be okay."

"Murphy!" she yelled.

"Wendy, he always comes back."

"Not always."

"When was the last time he ran away?"

"Fuck off, will you? I'm just trying to find my dog!" Wendy sloshed toward the shore, Rebecca close behind.

They searched the beach for a while and headed down a trail that circled the lake. Wendy knew, most likely, Murphy wasn't keeping to the path. The woods were deep. Wendy imagined Murphy whimpering and bleeding, maybe having gotten stung by something. Maybe many things. She imagined him hanging limply in the jaws of a massive bear. Or breathing heavily, bones broken and sticking out of his fur.

Wendy increased her pace. Rebecca kept up but stayed fifty feet or so behind. She wanted to give Wendy space to search and feel and fear.

The two women had made it halfway around the lake before running into Tim and his friends. Murphy and a teenage girl were splashing around in the water, wrestling over a large stick.

At the sight of his owner, Murphy splashed out of the lake and ran up to Wendy. She took his big head in her hands and gently tousled his ears. Murphy panted with delight.

"Have you had the dog this whole time?" Rebecca asked Tim.

"We took him for a walk. We were going to bring him right back."

"Do you realize how worried we've been?" Rebecca yelled at her son. "What the fuck were you thinking?"

Murphy's tail wagged. It was all excitement to him.

"Let's go home," Wendy said, turning toward the trail.

"Hey!" Rebecca called out to her. "You going to be okay?"

"I'll be fine."

"You want me to come with you?"

"No. I just need to be alone with my dog for a while."

"Okay. Love you!" she yelled.

Wendy didn't acknowledge Rebecca. She kept walking, leading Murphy away. She walked so fast nobody would have kept up with her.

Wendy was sweating and exhausted by the time she got back to the car. She turned the air conditioning on, she and Murphy taking in the cool air as they drove home.

HOLY WATER

GRANDMAFACE CAME OVER with the elderly dog, Magnus. It wasn't doing well. Both its eyes had fallen out. There were more bandages. Flies hovered around its backside.

Murphy was still happy to see his friend, though.

Magnus lay on the living room floor, drooling and coughing. Murphy ran around, finding socks and toys and pillows, bringing them over to his friend.

"You want a beer?" Wendy said.

"Sure," Grandmaface nodded.

She skipped to the kitchen and came back with two fancy microbrews she had bought at a brewery in Tomok. She also grabbed some lukewarm pizza.

They drank and watched the dogs.

"Do you think they love each other?" Wendy asked. "I mean, this is like a Hallmark card."

"A really gross Hallmark card."

"All hallmark cards are gross," Wendy said. "Holy shit, look. They're humping now."

"I don't think Magnus is humping back much. Just sort of taking it."

"They're totally dating."

"I don't know if Magnus would ever be monogamous. You think Murphy knows that?"

"Murphy is open-minded," Wendy said. "Very open-minded."

LENT

"I love these fries," Wendy said. "The Rosy Cheek Diner has the best fries. I love how they're accordion-shaped. It's so random."

"I used to have an outty belly button. It looked like that fry," Grandmaface said.

"That's awesome. What happened to it?"

"Lots of stuff."

"Do you still have it?"

"My grandmother kept it. She collected all our belly buttons."

"Shit. She died a while ago though. Who has them now?"

"I don't know. I think they went to a lab somewhere to be studied."

"Belly button science. Of course."

"I don't know."

"You know what's weird?" Wendy said. "This hasn't ruined my appetite. Like, at all. I'm still loving these fries."

"Do you want to keep looking for the whale later?"

"No, I think I'm over the whole whale thing."

"I think we should keep looking. Just to say we gave it our all."

"I think I did give it my all. Or I gave it something at least. Hey, maybe your mom has the belly buttons."

"I don't think so. My grandmother didn't like my mom much."

"I always wanted grandparents. But my parents hate them. They say they're bad people and shit. My parents are awful and they have the worst taste. So who knows, maybe my grandparents are awesome."

"I didn't like living with my grandmother. It was dirty in there and everything felt sweaty. She was a hoarder. The state didn't like me living there either, so when I was twelve I moved in with my Uncle Greg. He was a religious nut, and we had to go to church a lot. But at least everything was really clean."

"That was the guy that spanked us, right?"

"He was old-fashioned. But clean. I just remember loving how clean his house felt."

"You do love clean."

"I do. I respect what goes in to cleaning things."

"Is my place clean?"

"It's very clean," he said.

"That's 'cause once a week I smoke weed and then I clean everything. Cleaning things on weed is really fun. It's an unexplainable phenomenon."

"People who smoke weed too much remind me of my grandmother," he said. "She never smoked weed. But people who do remind me of her."

"Your grandma was a yeller," Wendy said. "I remember she yelled a lot."

"She didn't yell that much."

"Did too."

"No, you're wrong."

"Hey," Wendy said, "you know what I think is fucked up? If I took my shirt off right now, how long do you think it would take for someone to notice?"

"Not long."

"I think it would take a while. Let's find out. Let's do some science. Let's conduct some research."

"Stop fucking around. God fucking damn it, Wendy," Grandmaface said.

"Why are you so angry? I just wanted to test a theory."

"You push things too much. You want things to be exciting, but you're too pushy about it. You can't be pushy with that sort of thing."

"Look who's talking, Mr. Whale Hunter."

"That's different. Curiosity is a good way to have things happen. It's natural. It's clean. I don't know what goes on in you whenever you force yourself to do awkward things, Wendy. But it feels bad to me."

"What about the grilled chicken you stole?"

"What about it?"

"You sometimes just invade random picnics."

"That's 'cause I get hungry."

"You're so full of shit."

"It's different."

Wendy stared at her friend. "I get curious sometimes."

"I know."

"I really did want to see that whale."

"I know you did."

"I love whales. They're fucking huge."

"It was pretty great. I'm sorry I couldn't find it for you."

"I love whales."

"I didn't mean to upset you."

"You didn't."

"You're acting upset."

"I'm acting annoyed 'cause you are being annoying."

"I just didn't want you to get in trouble," Grandmaface said.
"Bullshit."

He took off his shirt. His body was surprisingly muscular.
"You happy now?"

"Holy shit!" Wendy said, laughing.

"Do I have to spin it around my head?"

"Grandmaface!" Rosy, the owner of the diner, yelled. "Put your fucking shirt back on!"

He looked to Wendy.

"I won't put it back on until you say it's okay."

Wendy couldn't stop laughing.

Rosy kept yelling at him.

"Put it back on," Wendy laughed.

He put the shirt back on.

"Grandmaface, that was great. It was better than music. You just reinvented laughter."

"Really? I feel like I just traumatized everyone."

"Yeah, but in a good way."

"You know what I miss?" he said.

"No clue. What do you miss?"

"I miss stretch marks."

"What do you mean? You were never fat."

"No, on women. I remember the first boobies I ever saw had these lava colored stretch marks all over them."

"I've never had any stretch marks," Wendy confessed.

"I didn't like them at first," he said. "Now I miss them."

"I would love to have just one stretch mark. Just one tiny stretch mark."

"I don't know why you don't. You eat way too much pizza."

"I know. I really do. I wish they had pizza here. Why don't diners ever have pizza? It seems like something they should have."

"I agree, wholeheartedly."

"I have so many ideas!" Wendy yelled, her face pointed at the dingy tiles of the diner ceiling.

"You do."

"I have so many ideas. I'm just full of them."

"Like what?" asked Grandmaface.

73

"Like we should go to the movies tonight. Boom! Best idea ever. And now I have just given that idea to you. Do what thou wilst with it."

"I don't really watch many movies."

"What? Movies are fun! I like laughing all loud and having people get uncomfortable. I love it when they tell me to 'shhh.' There is so much thought put into one tiny 'shhh'."

"I like the movie theater," Grandmaface said. "I just don't like movies. I don't like how they use the same actors over and over. I watch that Bill Murray guy in *Groundhog Day*, then next thing I know he's a Ghostbuster. That doesn't make any sense to me. And he acts the same in both movies. I just don't get it. Why do they use the same actors over and over like that?"

"People like them."

"It's too distracting for me."

"Actually that is weird, now that I think about it."

"Didn't mean to ruin movies for you."

"It's okay. They're too expensive anyway."

Wendy plucked some fries from her plate.

"You find a roommate yet?" Grandmaface asked.

"No, my dad's really on my ass about it too." Wendy chewed. "He's driving me nuts. Hey, would you like to move in?"

"Sure, I just gotta ask my girlfriend."

"The young-looking girl?"

"No, the other one."

Wendy's eyes widened.

"What do you mean?" she asked. "You have two girlfriends?"

He nodded.

"I actually have another girlfriend. But we don't like living to-gether really. Things haven't been going well."

"What do you mean?"

"She's a good woman. But she watches too much TV. And she makes the place look like a nursing home."

"That sounds kinda cozy."

"It can be. It can also feel unnatural."

"Wait a minute, Grandmaface. So who is this lady? Do I know her?"

"She's older."

"Like how much."

"Old."

"Like old-old?"

"She's old."

"Where does she live now?"

"Harmony Commons."

"That's an assisted living community."

"I guess you could call it that."

"Dude, your place probably looks like a nursing home because it *is* a fucking nursing home."

"It's technically assisted living. Not a nursing home."

"Do they know that you aren't actually old?" Wendy asked. "I mean, do they realize you just have a wrinkly face, but that you are in your thirties."

"I don't know. They like me. I had one of the ladies give me a bath once."

"That's so messed up."

"It was nice."

"But your body is fully normal. I just saw it. You are ripped. How could she not tell that you are young?"

"Don't know. Maybe she did know."

"You think she knew you were normal, but bathed you anyway."

"What do you mean by normal? Do you mean not old?"

"I'm just trying to figure out how you've been living in this place!"

"I like Gretchen. She's a good woman. Things have been hard since we moved in there."

"So her name's Gretchen. That's a classic old lady name. You two have sex?"

"Not often. We make out when I'm really drunk. But her body's in pretty rough shape. And she pisses herself a lot."

"Is that hot?"

"It's warm. Piss is warm usually."

"No, I mean, is it sexy?"

"Sometimes."

Wendy laughed.

"This is so wild," she said.

"It's not really working out between us. That's why I was thinking of moving in with you."

"This is blowing my mind. Is your girlfriend senile?"

"She remembers some things."

"Gross."

"Hey, watch what you say about her. She's a good one."

"Sorry. Just . . . it's so weird. Does the young one know about the old one?"

"She met her. She thinks it's my grandma. She's even seen us make out. She just thinks I'm being a really nice, really affection-ate grandson."

"That's so fucking nuts. So you get both ends of the spectrum."

"Of what spectrum?"

"Of life, I guess. It's the circle of life. Like that song from *The Lion King*. Which is playing at the Gibous Theater, by the way. Holy shit!" Wendy grabbed Grandamaface's arm. "We should see that. It's fate."

"Don't like lion movies."

"Who doesn't like lion movies? Are lion movies even a thing for people not to like?"

"I just don't like them."

"I still can't believe you have two girlfriends. Why aren't you moving in with the younger one?"

"She's too young. Have you ever seen the way twenty-year-olds live? I would rather live in a nursing home."

"That is so true."

"Keep this between us, okay? I don't want people gossiping about my love life."

"I promise I won't tell anyone."

CALL TO WORSHIP

WENDY TOOK MURPHY to visit Magnus.

Ray made Wendy a Hot Pocket, and she sat on the couch watching Murphy lick and sniff his friend's body. Magnus, the poor old dog, seemed particularly out of it that day.

"He's dead," Ray said.

"What do you mean?"

"He died. Last night."

"Of what?"

"Lots of stuff."

"And you just left him on the floor like this?"

"For the time being."

Murphy lay down next to his old buddy. They lay together in the sun that filtered through the living room window for a long while.

HYMN OF PRAISE

A FUNERAL FOR Magnus was held a couple of weeks later. It was still unseasonably warm, and people spent the service theorizing about global warming.

After the funeral, Grandmaface and Wendy took Murphy to the park.

"Thanks for waiting on this whole moving thing," Wendy said. "I've just wanted some alone time. You know, so the dog could heal."

"I understand."

"How's the nursing home?"

"Food's been good."

"Really?"

"Well, I like it."

"You can move in next week. You know, if you want."

"Thanks. It'll be good to get out of there."

"Heard a blizzard is coming."

"No way."

"It's true."

"It's so warm out though."

PRAYER OF ADORATION

GRANDMAFACE WOKE UP and found a woman in his room. She was wearing pink scrubs with pictures of Minnie Mouse on them. She was dressing Gretchen. When she bent over to change Gretchen's shoes her thong underwear showed. It was blue and looked like the edge of a waterfall.

"Morning. We're having eggs for breakfast," she said.

Grandmaface smiled and got out of bed, pulling his robe on.

He headed down the hall to check on the puzzle he had left in the common area.

His buddy Craig was there. The old man had bruises covering half his face from his last fall. He looked gentle and tired.

"How you doing, buddy?" Grandmaface said.

"No good. I have to fix this thing," Craig said, gesturing to the puzzle.

"It has a lot of pieces."

"That's for sure. Some fit in just fine. The rest, not so well. I don't know who's in charge of it. Certainly isn't me."

"You want my help?"

Craig shook his head, his eyes scanning the tabletop.

Grandmaface could tell he wanted to be left alone.

OLD TESTAMENT READING

AT AROUND SIX A.M. Wendy gave up on sleep.

She walked out into the backyard and saw the two old grey-hounds humping. They looked especially old that morning, and for some reason she felt angry.

Wendy chased the dogs around the house and into the street. She watched them head to the neighbor's yard, where they began humping again.

She stood in her front yard for a bit, smoking a cigarette. Day-lilies had sprung up, surrounding her porch. Her house needed to be painted. Even in the early morning light she could see the poor shape her home was in.

She couldn't stand to be near it. She needed to get away from it all.

It was Sunday. Church happened on Sundays. She wanted to go. She wanted to see her friend. She hadn't talked to Rebecca in a while. And she was sure her policy on church hadn't changed.

Wendy brought a baggy hooded sweatshirt to hide her face. She left the car in the driveway and set off walking in the direction of the church. It was a long walk, but Wendy figured walking all that way earned her the right to attend the service. To cross the boundary her friend had set up. To act needy in this way.

"Come on, Murphy!" she said. "We are going to church."

As soon as she stepped out the front door Wendy started to feel better. The fresh air tasted sweet and harsh, and there was a lot of it.

PRAYER OF CONFESSION DONE IN UNISON

BREAKFAST AT HARMONY Commons Assisted Living Community was good. Grandmaface loved the scrambled eggs.

He told the staff about how he was moving out. They were proud of him. One of the resident assistants flirted with him.

"We should get a drink some time. Party a little," the woman suggested.

"Maybe," Grandmaface said, scooping a forkful of eggs into his mouth.

"I like to dance. You dance?"

"Not much."

"But you can move around and pretend you are dancing?"

"I could do that."

"Perfect."

He spent the next hour walking around, saying goodbye.

In the common area was a screen that played a video of a flickering fireplace. Grandmaface walked in to find his friend Rooster peeing on it.

"What you up to, Rooster?"

"Nothing. Just walking around. I'm good at that."

"You are good at that," Grandmaface agreed.

"You work here?" the man asked.

"No, I live here. But I'm leaving."

"I live in Burtonsville. This Burtonsville?"

"It is."

"Well, I'll be."

They both smiled.

Grandmaface wanted badly to hug the man, but he walked away.

WORD OF COMFORT

REBECCA'S CHURCH WAS in a town called Lud, an hour or so drive from Burtonsville. Lud was a small town. It looked boarded up for the most part, and there were a few churches in town. Most of them looked like they were in rough shape. One had a bunch of cars in the parking lot.

Wendy and her dog walked in. She found a seat in the back row. Her hood was up, hiding her face.

THE STEEPLE

THE LIGHTS DIMMED. Wendy didn't know that happened at church. She thought that was a movie theater thing.

A spotlight shone onto the stage at the front of the church. Was it called a stage in church? Wendy didn't know. She felt out of her element. The place smelled like sunshine and dust.

Rebecca walked out, wincing at the lights like they were God's horrible morning breath.

"Thank you for coming," she said.

"Thank you for having us," the congregation responded.

"You may stand."

AFFIRMATION OF FAITH

WHEN THEY WERE done with the hymns the congregations sat back down. Pastor Rebecca began to deliver the sermon.

"I don't know what prayer is," she said. "I have never really understood it. It just seems strange. But when I was young I drank too much. And I didn't know how to stop. So I would walk. And stop places, and drink. And then walk more. And drink more. Sometimes I woke in strange places. I would force myself up and walk more. My feet hurt but I kept walking. I would fall asleep in parks and in people's houses, and under bridges, and I would feel tired and sore and sick, but I would force myself up and walk more. And I don't know what prayer is. I really don't. I have no idea what prayer is. But when I was young I walked and got drunk and walked until I was sober. Then I drank more, and I woke up in strange places. And I wanted to quit drinking. But I couldn't. I just couldn't do it. I ruined my marriage. I hurt my kid. I wanted to quit. I just couldn't do it. But I could walk. I could always walk. I would drink and I would walk. I don't know what prayer is. But I used to walk around. It felt important to walk. And I still walk. I still walk as much as I can."

The minister started humming.

Then the congregation started humming.

It sounded sexual. Wendy was crying. The sermon was strange but her memory of Rebecca's drunken days stirred her. She missed that version of her friend, yet at the same time she was glad they were over. She was glad her friend was sober.

THE WAY THE LIGHT TRAVELS THROUGH THE STAINED GLASS

REVEREND REBECCA WALKED away from the lectern and stood behind the altar. The congregation began pulling black garbage bags out of bags and pockets, draping them over their fronts. Wendy didn't have a trash bag and asked the person next to her if she wanted to share hers. The woman didn't respond.

A man in a long robe walked up to the altar carrying a large snapping turtle. He placed the turtle on the table.

Pastor Rebecca reached under the altar and pulled out a giant mallet.

"Lord! Stop hiding your head in your body so we can stop hiding ours!"

"AMEN!" the congregation called out.

Pastor Rebecca slammed the massive mallet onto the turtle, its shell exploding. Impossible amounts of guts and blood sprayed the crowd, and the people gasped and laughed.

Wendy caught a piece of grime in her mouth and spit it out. She gagged and dry heaved.

She looked around.

The whole place was covered in slime.

Another turtle was brought to the altar.

"REJOICE!" Pastor Rebecca yelled.

She brought the mallet down on the turtle, covering the congregation in slime.

BAD
DIRECTIONS

ONE

HELEN ROLLED DOWN her window and felt the cool air blow through her hair. She squinted and looked over the farmland. There were huge puddles in the fields. They looked as deep as lakes. Some of the puddles surrounded small, fragile homes. Helen liked the puddles, but she felt bad about it because she knew they made life hard for the farmers.

Her husband, Keith, drove. She caught him picking his nose. She made a comment. He got annoyed and ate the booger to taunt her.

"You're such a dweeb," she said.

He ignored her.

Keith fidgeted with the GPS as he drove. Helen hated that. It made her nervous. It was dangerous. It was just as bad as texting while driving. But she let it go because the roads were so empty and so flat and so straight.

She rolled the window down and smelled cool, wet air.

Ahead there were two girls walking down the street. They were young and wearing nothing but bathing suits, drenched from the rainstorm. Helen caught her husband staring. She laughed and rolled her eyes.

Helen didn't know where they were going. Keith told her it was a surprise. They had driven through the night and into the day and they were tired. Sometimes it felt sweet to be tired together like that. Still, it was getting late again and the weather app on her cell phone said the storm was going to pick up again. It showed a tornado watch.

Keith looked a motel up on the GPS. Helen didn't understand why he still used that thing. It was ancient. She had taken to calling it "Father Time." It was that old.

"Father Time barely works anymore," she said. "My phone has an app that can find a nice place."

"It works fine," he said. "I like using this old thing. Relax."

"I am relaxed," she said.

"In one quarter mile, turn right," the machine said.

"In eight hundred feet, turn right," it said.

"I hate that thing's voice," Helen said.

"Calm down," Keith said.

"Turn right," it said.

Keith missed the next turn.

"Recalculating," the machine said.

"Turn right in five miles," it said.

They drove by an old bar named "Pudgy's." Helen snickered. She loved how unashamed of being fat the Midwest was. Back where they were from, everything needed to be healthy or, at the very least, look healthy. Even the burger joints felt like health spas. It was nice to get away from all that.

Helen and Keith met going to college in upstate New York. Most students didn't leave campus. They considered the countryside near the school to be hilljacked. Deranged rednecks lurked in those mountains waiting to find college kids and do horrible things to them. But Keith and Helen liked to drive around and find rundown diners and eat burgers and feel lost together. They weren't as paranoid as their classmates, and they were proud of it.

"Turn right in one quarter of a mile," the machine said.

TWO

THEY DROVE BY another goofy-looking dive. "THE CHUNK." It advertised good beer and food on the sign.

Helen was hungry. She asked Keith to pull over.

He seemed annoyed but turned around.

"Recalculating," Father Time said.

"Oh shut up," Helen said.

"Make a U-turn when possible," the machine said.

They pulled into a dirt driveway and got out of the car.

"This place looks hilarious," Helen said.

Once they walked in, they realized they had made a mistake. Helen could tell Keith wanted to turn around and leave, so she found a seat and told the elderly bartender she wanted a beer. Keith grunted and sat next to her on the wobbly stool.

"What kind?" the old woman asked.

"Oh, you know what I'm in the mood for? I would love a real dark stout."

"What's that, like a Guinness? We don't have that. We got Budweiser and some Becks and Miller and some other stuff."

"A Bud Light please," she said.

The bartender looked at a beady-eyed man at the end of the bar and they both laughed. Then she reached under the bar and handed the bottle of Bud Light to Helen.

"Thank you," she said.

"Don't mention it."

The bottle was warm but Helen drank it anyway.

Keith didn't order a beer.

Helen gave Keith a sympathetic smile. Then she asked the bartender if they had any food.

"Food. Well, we got some chips and we got microwavable pizza."

"You like pizza," Helen said.

Keith shook his head.

"I'm okay," he said. "Thanks anyway, ma'am."

Keith leaned in, close to Helen. She thought he was going to kiss and flirt a little. Instead, he scolded her and told her he wanted to get back on the road.

THREE

"TURN RIGHT IN eight hundred feet," the machine said.

Keith made the turn.

It was still light out. Still early. Sorta. Since she hadn't slept the night before, it felt very late. But Helen reminded herself to just relax and not get grumpy.

She saw two girls walking down the street. They were in bathing suits. She laughed.

"Those can't be the same girls," she said. "Is walking around in your bathing suit, like, a thing in the Midwest? I thought it was supposed to be all old fashioned out here."

Keith didn't respond.

"We should get some snacks and go for a hike," she said. "Have a picnic."

"I don't think there is anywhere to hike around here," Keith said. "Besides, look at that sky."

"It's looked like that all day and we've seen nothing but a little rain."

"If I see anywhere to hike, I'll pull over."

"Hey, honey, how far away did it say this motel was?"

"Ten miles."

"You sure? We've been driving for more than ten miles."

"I don't know, Helen. We'll get there soon. Besides, we've gotten side-tracked looking for food."

"Maybe we'll just find someplace near the motel."

"I guess."

FOUR

HELEN GOT IN the back seat and undressed.

"What are you doing?" Keith said.

"Pull over," she said.

She spread her legs so he could see her pussy in the rearview mirror.

"Not right now," he said. "I'm not in the mood, like, at all."

"It's okay," Helen said.

She played with herself a little but got bored.

She looked through her purse, found a pipe, and smoked a little shabby weed. She got stoned and sleepy.

FIVE

THE CAR HIT a bump and Helen woke up.

She looked out the window at the fading light and the corn-fields. There were small patches of forest in the distance. She wondered about the animals hiding there.

"What time is it?" she said.

"We'll be there soon," he said.

She had forgotten about the motel and GPS.

Why was it taking them so long?

That GPS had no idea what was going on.

"Are we there yet?"

Keith didn't respond.

"Turn right in eight hundred feet," the machine said.

He made the turn.

"You will reach destination in one mile, on right."

They drove a mile and stopped, but there was nothing on either side of the road except prefab houses and muddy fields.

"Strange," Keith said.

"That thing is broken," Helen said. "Stupid thing."

"What thing?"

"That GPS," she said. "Father Time."

"I don't like when you call it that. Please stop. It's a good GPS and it's working fine. This motel probably just closed recently."

"Motel? What motel? I see nothing but cornfields."

Helen got out of the car and stretched. Her shirt lifted. She could feel fresh air on her exposed belly.

She looked up and down the road to make sure no cars were coming. Then she pulled down her panties, squatted, and pissed.

While she was mid-pee, she heard a squeal. She looked over and saw two animals humping. She thought it was two dogs. Well, one of them was a dog but the other animal was a raccoon. And the dog's dick looked peculiar. It had huge balls. Absolutely huge balls. They were wrinkled and pink like her husband's.

After she finished peeing she got back in the car.

"Can dogs and raccoons mate?" she said.

"Anything is possible," Keith said.

He started the car and turned back onto the road.

"Where are we going now?" she asked.

He explained that he had found a new motel. One that actually existed. The GPS said it was only fifteen miles away.

She could still see the animals mating in the rearview window.

She wondered if raccoons could have an orgasm. I'll have to google that when I get home, she thought.

SIX

HELEN FELL BACK asleep. When she woke up the light seemed strange.

She looked at her cell phone. It was morning.

"What's going on?" she said.

"Now calm down. You fell asleep and you looked cozy enough and I wanted to keep driving."

"So you didn't find the motel?"

"Well, I found a different one. It's a little farther away."

"Baby, aren't you tired?"

His eyes were bloodshot and he smelled like balls.

"I'm fine," he said.

They continued down the road.

There was another set of girls on the street. They were wearing nothing but bathing suits.

This is too messed up, Helen thought. I shouldn't have smoked so much weed.

Keith slowed down.

The girls were goofing around and laughing so loud Helen and Keith could hear them in the car.

One gave the other a wedgie.

Keith smiled.

"Such wonderful senses of humor," he said.

SEVEN

THE GPS INSTRUCTED them to take a right, then another right, then another.

They passed the girls again. The same girls as before. The one girl still had her bathing suit wedged up her ass.

"This is ridiculous," Helen said. "Baby, that thing isn't working."

"It's working. I just set it to backroads only."

The machine directed them to take a right, then another. Then another. It had directed them down different roads, but they were still moving in a circle.

They drove up to the girls again.

Again, Keith slowed down.

The girls noticed.

They shouted things and gave him the finger and laughed.

He laughed too.

They shook their butts at them.

One was chubby and had a lot of butt.

"Those girls are gross," Helen said.

"No, your attitude is gross. I am trying to take us on a nice little adventure but you are ruining it by getting all uptight."

"I am not uptight."

"Saying you are not uptight is a very uptight thing to say."

"Is not. Honey, I just think we have been driving for too long, okay? I'm hungry."

"You are such a nag."

"Am not."

"Are too."

"Am not."

EIGHT

THEY DROVE THROUGH a small town. Helen thought it was cute, like Cooperstown. Keith used to love to visit Cooperstown and visit the Baseball Hall of Fame. This was back when he was a baseball fanatic. This was back before he got all new-agey and chubby. She didn't mind the chubbiness. She had a boyfriend in high school who was chubby. They used to have really fun sex. She liked to suck on his man boobs. She wished Keith could be more playful and let her do silly, kinky things to his man boobs. But he wasn't.

Still, it was nice. She liked having all that weight on top of her and he got so warm while they slept. No, the chubbiness was not what bothered her. It was his laziness. He was always saying he was meditating, and that this was the only form of exercise he allowed. Sometimes he would do yoga, but the only position he liked was happy baby, which just looked like he was rolling around on the ground.

Everything was some form of meditation. He had even invented a new form of meditation called internet meditation. It simply involved surfing the web for hours. That's all. At least there was cleaning meditation. That was nice. The house was immaculate. She liked that.

But then he started taunting her for not having the same spiritual longing. So she started doing some of these meditations with him. She even did internet meditation, which usually involved her stalking ex-boyfriends on Facebook.

NINE

THEY STOPPED AT a red light.

A truck pulled up next to them. The driver and Helen made eye contact. He smiled at her. She did not smile back. The truck driver started growling at her. While he growled he fondled his own man boobs.

"This guy's really creeping me out," she said.

"Stop being such a snob," Keith said.

"What the fuck? Look at this guy. He's crazy."

"If he was listening to Lady Gaga you two would be best friends."

"What the fuck are you talking about? That doesn't even make sense."

The light turned green. The truck sped off.

"Feeling better now?" Keith said.

"Fuck off. You can be so mean."

TEN

THEY DROVE THROUGH another town. This one was bigger. More of a small city.

But it was also incredibly empty.

There were stray dogs everywhere. It reminded her of the reservations they had driven though years before when they were on their big cross country trip. Keith loved the stray dogs. He wanted to pet them all and get licked by them and play tug of war with socks. He loved them. He thought each stray was the most adorable thing he had ever seen.

At the time, Helen was annoyed. She didn't want a dog. She thought they made life too complicated. They would leave clumps of fur on the furniture and they got sick and they died. She didn't want a dog, let alone a stray. But now she sorta wished she had gotten a dog back then. She cherished the memory of those strays. She missed that side of her husband.

Keith did not seem as into the dogs in that town or little city or whatever it was. He almost hit one that darted across the road. He cursed at the thing.

It stood up on its hind legs and hissed at him.

Helen realized it wasn't a dog at all. It was a raccoon. Half the

110

animals wandering around the city were raccoons.

As they were driving out of town they saw several motels. Helen wanted to pull over and rest. Keith refused.

ELEVEN

MORE GIRLS IN bathing suits.

"It looks like the same girls," Helen said.

"That's impossible."

"I'm telling you, it's the same girls."

"I highly doubt it."

They came to another town.

They found a restaurant and got some dinner. She had mozzarella cheese sticks wrapped in fried wontons. Her mood lifted. These were incredible cheese sticks. All the food made her tired though.

When she got in the car she checked the GPS to see their estimated time of arrival. It said they should be there at 40000000000 p.m.

"What the hell is going on?" she said.

"Its fine. Just a little glitchy, that's all."

"I hope you're right."

TWELVE

"I'M BORED," she said.

He reached in the back and grabbed one of his books. It was the last one he had self-published. It was about how he quit being a gym teacher to inspire the world to be more spiritual or whatever. She had already read it so many times. She was his editor. Well, sort of. She didn't really know what she was doing and every time she even looked at the book she felt embarrassed. There were so many typos and ridiculous-looking sentences.

Still, she pretended to read the book as they drove.

They drove by more cornfields, then more teenage girls wearing nothing but bikinis. Or maybe they were the same girls. That idea felt crushing to her. She closed her eyes and tried not to think about it.

"I hope we are going the right way . . ." she heard Keith say.

"There is no wrong direction," the GPS said.

"I just can't handle how uptight my wife gets on these trips!"

"Chances are you can probably solve your problem with kindness or compassion or gratitude. Choose one, choose them all."

She recognized that line. It was from one of his books. Had Keith programmed the GPS to give himself advice or had he stolen these lines from that stupid machine? No, it couldn't be the GPS. What a stupid idea. It was probably just one of his new-agey buddies talking on speakerphone.

But that voice. So sassy, but monotone at the same time.

It was all in her head. She was sure of it.

"I know," Keith said. "It's just . . . it gets so hard . . ."

"There is no danger in opening your heart, unless you close it too soon."

The car was moving fast. She figured they were on a highway, which made her feel relieved. It would be easier to find a hotel from the highway. They could stay at a Best Western. Or better yet, a Hampton Inn. They have cookies at the front desk. She loved cookies.

The car swerved. She hit her head against the window. She cursed and groaned and looked at her husband.

He was not on his phone.

And they were not on the highway.

They raced through the woods. They were on a barely paved, twisted road. The tires squealed as they turned. Dust clouds burst open behind them.

"What's going on?" Helen said. "Keith, slow down. Please, baby, slow down. You're scaring me."

An animal darted into the middle of the road. A raccoon. It stood on its hind legs and hissed. It had a huge dick.

"KEITH, STOP!" she screamed.

They hit the raccoon. It exploded. Guts and slime and fur hit the windshield. The windshield wipers wiped hard, flinging grime to the side.

"WHAT THE FUCK!" Helen screamed.

For a moment, it felt like the car had lost control, but it suddenly righted itself.

"PLEASE STOP!" she yelled.

Finally, he took his foot off the accelerator. The car slowed down.

"What the hell is wrong with you?" she said.

He didn't look at her. He kept his eyes on the road.

"Sorry," he said. "I was just trying to make up for lost time."

THIRTEEN

"YOU DON'T NEED to search very far. Your life is a mystical experience," the GPS said.

"What did that thing just say?" Helen said. "Did you program it to say weird stuff?"

"The machine is more advanced than it seems," he told her.

They pulled over at a gas station.

Helen looked at her hands. She was so shaky. And her eyes felt crusty. She hadn't been blinking enough. She was still freaked out by that raccoon. She rolled her window down. She reached out and traced a line in the dried blood still covering the edges of the windshield.

She took a deep breath.

The gas station looked so elderly. The pumps were rusted and advertised only twenty-five cents a gallon.

An incredibly handsome and muscular man wearing nothing but overalls came out and pumped gas for them.

"Gas is getting so fucking expensive," Keith said.

"Trying is committing to the attempt. Persistence is committing to the goal. Choose wisely," the GPS said.

"What the fuck does that even mean?" Helen said.

"Maybe if you were more receptive to the mysteries of the universe, you would be more receptive to its answers," Keith said.

"Whatever."

Keith put the key in the ignition. The car came to life. Keith took a left out of the parking lot. They passed by an old farm house. It was late, but there was still a light on. Helen imagined an old man waking up early, getting ready for chores, enjoying the quiet.

FOURTEEN

KEITH PULLED OVER.

"What's wrong?" Helen asked. "Do we have a flat?"

Keith wouldn't look at her.

She turned and looked out the back window. It was dark, but she could see three figures moving toward the car. Three girls. All wearing bikinis. Lit only by the brake lights.

"What the fuck are you doing?" she asked him.

"Calm down," he said. "It's late. They're cold. And they need a ride."

"This is so fucked."

The back door opened and the girls piled in. They were laughing in a scandalous way teenage girls are so good at.

"Thank you so much for the ride," a girl with short blonde hair said. "It's so cold out there. I thought my tits were going to freeze off."

"Where are you girls headed?" Keith asked.

"I hope you don't mind," a girl said. "We're going to our friend Mandy's. It's kinda far away though."

"Just give me the address and I will type it into my GPS."

"Oh my God!" the pudgy one said. "You have a GPS?"

"Sure do!"

"That's awesome. Can I see it?"

He took the machine off its frame and handed it to the pudgy girl whose breasts barely fit inside her bikini top. Helen winced. That chunky bitch was going to get her titty sweat all over the GPS. Then Keith was going to touch it when using the GPS, and then he would touch her, inadvertently getting the teenager boob sweat on her. So gross.

"This is so fucking cool," the girls said.

As the girls looked over the machine, Keith pulled away. Helen sulked and looked out the window, hoping the situation would end shortly.

"You have all the power of the universe at your disposal," the GPS said.

The girls moaned.

"It's so smart," the blonde said.

The car shook. They were on a dirt road. Tall wildflowers scraped the edge of the car.

"Keith, where the fuck are we going?" Helen asked.

He ignored her.

"Keith, why the fuck are we in the middle of the woods?" she asked.

"Uh oh," one of the girls said.

They laughed.

"Take next right," the GPS said.

"Mmmmm. It gives such good directions," the pudgy one said.

She was breathing so heavily one of her breasts had popped out. Keith had his eyes glued on the rearview mirror.

"Keith, stop being an ass. You're freaking me out again," Helen said.

"You don't need to search very far," the GPS said. "Your life is a mystical experience."

Helen looked back and saw the blonde fingering her pudgy

friend. Their friend, a scrawny girl with long brown hair, held the GPS to her chest.

"What are you doing?" she said to the girls.

They ignored her.

"Take next left," the GPS said.

There was an old sign on a tree. It said PRIVATE PROPERTY. TRESPASSERS WILL BE SHOT.

"You are going the wrong way, Keith," Helen said. "We can't go down this road. It's trespassing."

"There is no wrong direction," the GPS said.

"Listen to the machine," Keith said.

He reached back and touched one of the girls' legs.

"You don't need to search very far. Your life is a mystical experience," the GPS said.

She looked in the backseat. The girls were almost completely nude. The car stank like teen pussy. Helen was at her wit's end.

"STOP!" she screamed. "ALL OF YOU NEED TO STOP!"

Everyone laughed. Even the GPS seemed to be enjoying her hissy fit.

"Trying is committing to the attempt. Persistence is committing to the goal. Choose wisely," the GPS said.

"It's so beautiful," the blonde moaned. "Your machine is so beautiful."

"I'm so sick of that thing!" Helen yelled.

She reached back and grabbed the GPS. As soon as she pulled it into the front seat and out of the girl's sweaty hands, the girls let out an ear-piercing hiss. The pudgy one lunged at her and bit her arm.

Helen screamed.

"GET HER OFF ME!"

She wouldn't let go.

"STOP! IT BURNS!" Helen yelled.

The other girls laughed.

"Endings are really beginnings in the eyes of the Divine," the GPS said.

Helen became dizzy.

"Please . . . stop . . ."

She could hear the girls laughing.

FIFTEEN

WHEN SHE CAME to, the girls were gone. They were still driving down the unpaved road. It was morning and the light was strange and cool.

Her left arm burned. She remembered being bit.

She tried to look at the wound but all she could see was a mound of bandages.

She tried to focus.

"KEITH!" she screamed.

"Yes, honey?"

"What happened to my arm?"

She held the stump in front of her.

"It got infected, sweetie, but the GPS helped. It told me how to amputate, step by step."

She started to nod off again.

A tear fell down her cheek.

She mumbled to herself as she lost consciousness.

SIXTEEN

"YOUR TIME HERE is finite. The longer you stay angry and upset, the less time you have for joy and wonder. Your call. Choose wisely."

Helen struggled to open her eyes.

"Morning, honey!" Keith said.

She felt her left arm. She held her stump and started to cry again.

Finally, she opened her eyes, let in the light.

They were still driving but weren't on a main road, or a back road, or even a dirt road. He was driving through the woods.

"I want to go home," she said.

"You don't need to search very far. Your life is a mystical experience," the GPS said.

Helen wept.

SEVENTEEN

WHEN SHE CAME to again, they were driving into the mouth of a large cave. It was dark, and large animals skittered into hiding when they saw the headlights.

"Endings are really beginnings in the eyes of the Divine," the GPS said.

They drove deep into the cave. The passage got so narrow she thought they were going to get stuck. The car sparked as its metal ground against wet rock.

Helen wept and held her stump.

EIGHTEEN

IT FELT LIKE they had been in the cave for hours. They barely had any gas. Soon the headlights and interior lights in the vehicle turned off. Had they run out of gas? They must have. But the car was still moving. She could feel it moving.

At times, it felt like they were floating. There was no sound. No engine humming. No animal fleeing. Though Keith couldn't see, the vehicle didn't scrape against the side of the cave anymore.

There was just the sound of the GPS, telling them where to go.

NINETEEN

FINALLY, LIGHT.

TWENTY

THEY PULLED OUT of the cave and into a forest. Soon, they were on a road paved with pine quills. The ride became less bumpy. They were on pavement now. Eventually they were on a road again. And it was smooth and shiny black.

Helen saw something in the distance. A sign.

Shady Pine Motel, six miles ahead.

TWENTY-ONE

"YOU HAVE REACHED your destination," the GPS said.

They pulled into the motel. Keith went into the office. When he came out, he had a set of keys in his hand.

"We are in room seven," he said.

He drove them over to the room. He got out, popped the trunk, and took out their bags.

"Aren't you coming?" he asked.

"Just give me a moment," she said.

He walked into their room.

Helen stepped out of the car. She smelled the pines. She listened to the birds and the sounds of vehicles driving by.

She looked at her stump.

She got into the driver's side, got in the car, and drove away.

TWENTY-TWO

AS SHE DROVE, she wept.

"I don't know where to go," she said to herself.

"Take a right in point five miles," the GPS said.

She drove down the road and then took the right.

"Endings are really beginnings in the eyes of the Divine," the GPS said.

"So true," she said to herself.

The GPS told her to continue down that road for ten more miles. She drove at a leisurely pace.

In the distance, she saw someone standing at the side of the rode. As she got closer, she saw that it was a man. He was shirtless. He wore only a pair of cut-off jean shorts so tiny it looked like his shlong could fall out at any second. His massive pecs glistened in the sun. His triceps almost shattered her mind. They seemed to contain such power.

He stuck his thumb out and smiled.

She drove by the man. The GPS changed their route. It took her down a series of mangled roads, and then brought her back onto that main route so she could see the shirtless hitchhiker again.

WITCH
TITTIES

I GOT OUT of the car and scratched my giant balls. They felt awe-some. No wonder chicks loved to play with them so much. God-damn, I was so handsome. I was born to hunt beaver. But, to be honest, that got me in trouble. That got me a baby and that baby turned into a dweeb and now I had to go to the fucking school and talk to his fucking principal.

His school's principal was Miss Winterby. I used to fuck around with her sister back in the day. They were both gothy chicks. They said they were witches. I didn't care. Her bedroom smelled like a Hot Pocket and she didn't know how to kiss worth a shit, but she had nice pale boobies and she let me suck on them. One time she sprinkled some powder on my ball sack and said a spell or some sort of shit. It felt great. I came part way into the spell. Shot the load right onto her cheek. She didn't even mind. She just licked the wad off with her giant nerd tongue. Good times. Being young was a goddamn good time. I liked standing there looking at the place.

I was feeling all peaceful and sentimental and shit and then this fat ass security guard escorted a woman out of the school.

"I was just looking for my boy!" the woman yelled.

The guy apologized but told her she had to get going. I didn't recognize the lady at first. But when I got closer I realized it was

Donna Myre. Her husband, Roy, ran off with her son a week before. I knew Roy. And I was surprised he would just run off on such a fine piece of ass. And man, Donna was one fine piece of ass cake. I would blow out all her candles, if you know what I mean. There was no way Roy was ever getting an ass like that again. No way. The guy was a hopeless nerd.

It was a fluke he got with Donna in the first place. I guess some women have a fetish for tiny nerd cock. I didn't care. All I knew was that I wanted to put my worm in that apple butt. I wanted to wipe her tears away with my dick, if you know what I mean. I decided right then and there I was going to slam my meatness into Donna Myer. I wanted to bring her home. Show her the meat packing district, if you know what I mean. Sure, I would wait a week or so. Give some time for the grief to subside.

I waved to Donna as she walked by. She gave me the finger. The middle. She wanted it. She wanted my breakfast sausage all in her egg McMuffin.

I walked up to the guard.

"Hey big titties, I got an appointment," I said.

He growled. Apparently you didn't need to be very intelligent to get this job. Apparently you didn't even need to be verbal.

I walked down the hall. Found a bathroom. It was hilarious. The urinals were all tiny and low to the ground. I stood a good six feet away and took my dick out. My dick felt so good in my hand I ended up making myself hard. Real hard. I mean, I was like Thor's hammer down there. I started pissing. First, it hit the wall. I had to force my mighty meat rod downward, aim it toward the tiny urinal. The janitor came in and saw me pissing from all the way across the bathroom. I winked at the old man. He blushed and ran off.

After I was done pissing I walked down the hall. The place was abandoned. Lonely feeling. The only light came from the main office. I walked in. Told the secretary I had an appointment. She had me sit and wait for like twenty minutes. It was strange. Even though I was full grown and had an awesome dick and could kick anyone's ass, even though I didn't give a fuck in the long run about my kid's education or anything like that, I still felt like I was in trouble somehow. It was fucked.

Finally I got called into the principal's office. For a moment I was nervous but then I saw Miss Winterby. What a blob of nerd. I mean, she was a big lady. Had a nice ass though. A real big pile of ass. Ass mountain. That's what she had. And she wore way too much make-up and she had one of those things Indian chicks have on their forehead. No, it wasn't a bindi. It was bigger. It was more like a symbol. Like a snake with a dagger through it. Only it wasn't like a dagger but more like a tooth. Sorta.

"So how can I help you today, Mr. Harris?" she asked, acting real smug, like all new-agey chicks tend to.

"I'm here about my kid," I told her.

"Danny."

"Right. He's gotten too fat. Well, he's not fat fat. But he's chunky as hell and lazy. He's got these boobs. They are like female boobs but on a man. I think he got them from being so fat all the time."

"Manboobs."

"Right. Anyway. They ain't right. They ain't right at all. Having boobs is confusing for a boy. What if he ends up turning himself on? Or other boys start trying to suck on them? What if he gets titty fucked by some stud? I just can't imagine that would be very good for the little fat ass's self-esteem."

"I see," she said. "Have you considered putting him on a diet?"

"A diet? No. Diets are way too girly. That would be counterproductive. I'm trying to turn him into a man. A real man. With a big dick and ripped pecs and all that."

"Of course. So what do you suggest?" she asked.

"I suggest taking him out of all these English classes and these social studies and art and all that and putting him into gym class, all day long. Just for one year."

I was getting excited. And talking loud. It made Miss Winterby nervous. Nervous and horny. I could tell. She was all sweaty. Not like how all fat people are sweaty. Like that good, sexy sweat with pheromones in it and shit.

I stood up and turned my act up a notch.

"I want my boy strong, like his daddy."

I looked down at her. I rolled up my sleeve. Flexed.

"Look at this pile of shit. Look at this big ole pile of shit. You don't get this from studying the works of William Shakesqueer? No. You gotta go to the gym. You gotta play dodgeball. Purple people eater. Run laps and shit."

"It's so true," she said. "I've been pushing for more gym in the curriculum for years. Years."

"You have?"

She stood up. Walked up close to me. I could smell her pussy mushing around down there. Each step she took sounded like waves pummeling the shore.

"If only the rest of the staff were like you."

"Like me?"

She put her hand on my right pec. It was super hard that day. I had just come from the gym.

"I wish every teacher here was as strong and brave and durable and handsome as you. I want the kids to have people to look up to. Instead, I have a bunch of nerds."

"I hate nerds," I said.

"Me too."

"Hey, remember when I used to date your sister?"

She blushed. "Of course. I used to get so jealous."

And she put her face on that right pec. I flexed it. She laughed.

I didn't quite believe anything she was saying though. She was too artsy to be that into handsome men like me. There weren't any pictures of athletes on her office walls. She had weird tapestries and a painting of women dancing naked in the forest. No way this girl liked gym class as much as me. Still, I was willing to fill her tank as long as it helped my boy. I was a good dad. A damn fine dad.

So I grabbed her pudgy paw and led it down to penis town. She held it. She quivered. She was so excited I got worried she was going to pass out or something. Couldn't have that. So I took her hand away. And I started disrobing her.

For a big fat chick, she was not modest at all. And I liked that. She was fully comfortable with her big fat body. And she had this abnormality. Nothing too gross. But definitely weird. She had all these nipples. All over. It was like every glob of fat had a nipple at the end. Even her ass cheeks had nipples. I liked that. I wished all ass cheeks had nips on them. I got super turned on. I bent her over her desk and sucked on one of her ass nipples and jerked myself off. She moaned. I put my face in her ass. Tasted the ass sweat and the grime. Fatties have the assiest asses. I heard her moaning. Only she wasn't just moaning. She was chanting something. I pulled my face out of the ass cavern.

"What the fuck are you rambling about?" I asked.

She smiled. "Lie down on the desk, Mr. Harris," she said.

"You going to suck my dick?"

"Sure. If that's what you like."

"Who wouldn't like that?"

I got on her desk and took my jeans off. I wasn't wearing underpants. Nothing but boner under those jeans. She liked. It was big and fat just like her. She put it in her mouth. She knew how to work that tongue. She took it all in too. Gagged on it. And while she was gagging she kept chanting. I didn't know what that shit was about. She was probably just saying some weird yoga prayer. I didn't care. I let her suck on it.

I got a little bit woozy. I wanted to stop. Take a break. But a real man doesn't let a tummy ache hold him back from deep dicking a chick. So I persevered. I kept on burying my dong in that greasy poon tang.

She got on top. Started riding hard. My whole body started feeling weird and soft and fucked up. I didn't let her stop though. I let her ride it hard. As long as my dick was still rock hard and gigantic, I figured the game was still on.

"Ride it, ya big bitch," I mumbled.

She kept chanting all sorts of weird shit. She got excited as hell. Her body was dripping sweat. Then I saw her nipples getting real hard. I mean, like they were actually growing. Soon they looked like small penises.

"I'm coming!" she said. "Oh Mother Ishwan. Master of all dark magic. I'm coming so hard for you."

White stuff shot out of her nipples. It got all over me. It was really slimy and thick and it burned more than a little. I wanted to push her off but I was too weak. I couldn't even speak. All I could do was lie there and get hosed down by the big bitch.

I came to with my face pressed against the cool tile floor. My stomach ache was gone, but I didn't feel quite right. I got up. It looked like the middle school bathroom but the urinals weren't all small and shit. Then I looked at the mirror. I had changed. I wasn't the big dicked musclebound stud I was earlier that day. I was all small and scrawny. My dick was still a good size but, other than that, I looked like I used to back when I was like twelve years old.

The school security guard walked in. Guy looked like Idiot Mountain. Massive. Too massive to fuck with.

"Bro, what the fuck's going on?" I said.

He laughed.

He tossed me some clothes. Sweat pants. A wife beater.

I put them on. And he dragged me into the other room. I didn't fight back. Idiot Mountain was too big, too sweaty for a shrunken little stud like me to take on, that was for sure.

I looked around the room. It was dark. A strange smoky light lit the center of the room. I could see a circle of desks. That was it. I sat down. There were a bunch of kids sitting there, looking sad and confused. I asked them what was going on but they didn't answer.

I recognized one. It was Roy. I mean, it didn't look like full grown up adult Roy, it looked like Roy did back in the day. Back in middle school. I figured Miss Witch Titties shrunk him down too. Fuck.

I told him his wife had been looking for him. He started to cry.

A line of women in robes came out of the darkness. They stood behind us. I could smell their pussies.

"What the fuck's going on?" I asked. "What did you do to me? What is this place?"

One of them hissed at me. My nipples started to burn and I screamed. They laughed.

Finally the pain went away.

I looked up. Roy's kid, Kenny, was in the middle of the circle. Idiot Mountain grabbed Roy and put him with his kid.

Kenny growled at his father and Roy just wept.

It was hard to watch.

They started fighting.

The witches chanted as they grappled.

Kenny pinned his father onto the tile floor. He growled. Drool dripped out of his mouth and onto his father's face. Roy begged him to stop. But the boy just laughed. It was not a good laugh. It didn't sound happy or anything. It sounded mean.

Kenny head-butted his father hard. Right in the face. Blood came out of his nose and eye sockets. I think he had beaten his head open as well. A puddle of blood had gathered on the floor. He did it again and again. It was hard to watch. Usually I loved watching a good fight. But there was something about this that made me feel all freaked out inside.

Kenny got his father's face good and mashed up. He put his fingers into Roy's eyes and started plucking them out. I yelled for him to stop, but one of the witches grabbed my shoulder and an awful burning filled my body and it didn't stop until she let go.

Finally, the women dragged the body away and the boy stood up—victorious.

Victorious and confused.

The kid looked very confused.

One of the women told him to take a seat. He did what he was told.

Idiot Mountain dragged Roy's body into the darkness.

Another boy entered the center of the ring. It was Danny. My boy. The fat ass fruit of my loins. They had me stand up and face him.

"Danny, what's this shit all about? Where the fuck are we?"

"Fuck you, Dad," he said.

Smartass. Usually I would slap him silly for saying some shit like that, but the witches started chanting and then the kid punched me in the gut and the next thing I knew I was on the ground.

Kid could really hit. I was shocked.

"You better watch yourself, big titties, I ain't about to get my eyeball plucked out like Roy, so don't even . . ."

He ran up and slugged me. I took it. It hurt like a motherfucker, but I took it. I even gave him a little smile. And then hit him back. I gave him swift jabs to the gut and then, once he had toppled over, I kicked him right in his temple.

He rolled around on the ground, whimpering.

And those nasty witches kept chanting. There was something so pervy about it, like these ladies were getting a little too hot and bothered about my son rolling around on the floor looking pathetic.

I kneeled down and tried to help the boy up. He bit my hand. The dweeb. Who bites during a fight? Such a chick move.

I decked him.

He took it.

Then he got his one good shot in. Right in my nuts. I fell over.

Danny crawled away. I thought he was just being a pussy. But, no, the little fat ass genius was just positioning himself. He kicked me right in the nut sack. Real hard too. Two shots in the nuts. The boy was vicious and, within all the pain, I was starting to feel a strong sense of pride in the boy.

I stayed on the floor. Groaning. Danny got on top of me. Since that lady shrunk my manly body down, my own son was heavier than me. It was hard getting out from under him but I managed. I staggered away. He came at me and hit me in the back of the head.

It was a good hit. I got all dizzy and shit. But he hurt himself as well. He held his bloody knuckles and cried a little.

"You okay?" I asked. My voice cracked. I sounded all pubescent.

"Fuck you," he said.

He ran at me. I dodged him. He fell.

The kid crawled at me. He grabbed my leg and pulled me down.

The kid was crying. I grabbed him and held him close.

"Stop this shit," I said. "It's okay. I'm not mad."

He tried to break free. But I didn't let go of him. I held onto him. We both started weeping. We were having some fruity sentimental love thing. And it was kinda nice. I felt like I was in a Robin Williams' movie.

The chanting got intense. The ladies were really pissed off but I didn't care. My bones started to burn. Whatever spell they were casting on us made our whole bodies feel like an eyeball sprayed with mace. I held my boy closer. He was such a fat ass. So cuddly.

The witches closed in. They were hissing and drooling on us.

But we just held onto each other. Crying. We were crying like women at the end of *The Notebook*.

The women standing over us took their robes off. They had little penis-shaped nipples all over their bodies. And they were all fat. I couldn't tell them apart. The chanting got impossibly loud. It hurt my ears. White stuff shot out of their nipples. I couldn't tell if it was jizz or milk or both.

I held onto my son.

"Daddy," my boy said. "I'm scared."

"It's all right. You are going to be all right," I said to him.

The stuff kept pouring out of them.

The chanting turned into screaming.

We were in a puddle of white stuff.

Now blood was shooting out of the creepy bitches. Blood and this other skin-colored slimy shit. It was like they were melting. The puddle of blood and white stuff got deeper. We held our breaths.

It consumed us.

The screaming stopped.

Finally.

Everything felt calm.

I stood up. I helped my boy up.

We were still covered in slime.

The witches were gone.

I could see more clearly now. We were in a classroom.

I walked up to one of the windows and pulled up the shades. Light poured into the room. It felt warm and good.

"Hey, you okay?" I asked my son.

He stood there, covered in gunk. He didn't say anything. He was too freaked out.

"You'll be okay," I said.

The slime was up to our knees. I saw a skull floating in it. Didn't know who it belonged to. Could have been one of those witch ladies. Or it could have been one of the students.

"Love killed them," my son said. "We killed them with our love."

"Don't be such a girl," I said.

He laughed.

I walked up. Put my hand on his shoulder.

"You think you're ever going to get normal again?" he asked. "Are you going to turn into an adult again?"

"I don't know. Who knows? I figure, fuck it, right? All I know is I'm hungry."

We walked out of school. It smelled like September. You know. Dead leaves and shit. We walked into town and I thought about going back to high school and balling high school chicks. But I decided that would be awkward. 'Cause they would be my son's friends, and it might hurt the nerd's feelings. Then I decided, if I didn't change back, I could go to a different school and get tons of pussy there. That would work.

Neither of us talked much. We just walked and felt the slime on our bodies get all crusty.

The pizza place was closed. We sat out front on a bench and waited for it to open. I saw a woman walk by. She was big and wearing sweatpants. For a moment, I got nervous. Then I realized she was just a normal chick. She wasn't a witch. Shit. That whole deal gave me PTSD. Big ladies would always make me nervous.

Around eleven, Conca opened. We walked inside. The angry bald guy behind the counter smeared sauce on uncooked dough, then looked up at us.

"What the fuck happened to you two?" he asked.

We looked at each other.

"We fell in some mud," I said.

Then I ordered us some pizza.

My wallet was back at school, so Danny had to pay for everything. He was cool about it.

"Hey, aren't you kids supposed to be in school," the bald guy said.

"Fuck school," I said.

My son and I high-fived and laughed.

We took our pizza outside and ate slowly.

I felt good until I saw Roy's wife across the street. She seemed lost and confused and sad as shit. I got all messed up feeling inside. I guess there was always something to remind you what you have been through. I waved to her. She didn't wave back. I had no chance at fucking her now. I looked like a child. Or maybe she was into teenage cock and balls. That would be cool. Older chicks were hot as hell.

FIRST
DATE

ONE

LUCAS WORE OLD lady sunglasses. They were huge and he rarely took them off. They looked like virtual reality goggles for people who love napping. Some people told him they were granny terminator glasses. He didn't like that though. He didn't like talking about his glasses. "They are just glasses," he'd say.

Once he told his friend Rick why he loved the glasses so much. They were having a sleepover and watching a horror movie that had so much nudity in it. As always, Lucas had his sunglasses on and couldn't see the movie very well. So he became really bored and decided to finally open up about the glasses.

"I have a staring problem," he said. "It's really bad. You see, I am kinda a ladies man. Like I really love all sorts of ladies so much. I just love staring at ladies. But I don't want to creep them out. So I wear these glasses."

"I don't think it's working," Rick told him.

TWO

ONE AFTERNOON, DURING recess, Rick and Lucas were playing basketball with some friends. Of course, the sunglasses were a problem. Lucas couldn't see the ball.

"Can you take them off this one time?" Rick asked.

"It's lunch time," he said. "There are just too many ladies here. Can't you smell the romance in the air?"

"All I can smell is arm pits and Doritos."

Lucas laughed.

"Come on, dude," Rick said. "We're playing basketball right now. You haven't caught a single pass, man. You look ridiculous."

"It's hard to see the ball with these glasses on."

"That's what I'm saying. Take the fucking things off."

"No, I feel like I have trapped the spirit of hundreds of females in these glasses."

"That's so fucking creepy."

Rick reached for the glasses. Lucas dodged his buddy's sweaty talons.

"Come on, dude."

"Can you just relax?"

The two friends wrestled and tickled each other for a bit.

"Well, who are you staring at today?" Rick asked.

"It's not like that, man. It's not a creature of the week, like an *X-Files* episode."

"Don't be so sensitive about it, douche bucket. Just tell me who you've been staring at."

"I think her name's Nicole."

"The giant?"

"She is exceptionally tall."

"And she's a fucking stoner. And she wears the same pants like every day."

"She's a dreamer. Look at her right now. Probably thinking about all sorts of beautiful stuff."

"She's just really, really stoned," Rick said.

"Maybe."

"I can't deal with a girl that spends her entire day chewing on her shirt sleeve."

"Trust me. That's a sign of passion."

"Says who?"

"Says most therapists."

"You would know," Rick said.

"I'm not ashamed of the time I have spent with Dr. Grimboli."

They kept playing. Rick tried to pass to Lucas, but the ball hit him in his right forearm and he fell to the ground. Lucas was in a daze.

This kept happening. Rick became furious and threw the ball as hard as he could at Lucas, hitting the back of his head and knocking him to the ground.

"What the fuck?" Lucas said.

Somehow his glasses had stayed on so Rick couldn't see Lucas's tears.

THREE

IN BETWEEN CLASSES Rick tried to find Lucas and apologize. He ran into him after history but Lucas started crying again and ran off.

After school, Rick waited by the bike racks, hoping to run into Lucas. Usually, Lucas went this way on his walk home. But that day he must have chosen another route, maybe snuck out of the gym entrance.

By four the school felt empty and unwelcoming. He headed to the deli down the street. It was one of the few delis left in Sag Harbor. When he was little, the town had so many delis. Most of them had been turned into coffee shops or art galleries.

Usually old men sat outside on a bench and drank tall paper cups full of coffee. But that afternoon there were no old men. Instead, that Nicole girl was sitting there. She was chewing on her sleeve and looking gross, as usual.

"Do you have a cigarette?" she asked.

Rick shook his head.

"Well, at least I have this. I found this one butt on the ground," she said. "It's almost an entire cigarette. Should we just smoke it together?"

She talked to him like they were already close friends and this had an effect on him. Usually cigarettes annoyed him. He thought they smelled awful. The idea of smoking a cigarette found on the ground absolutely disgusted him. But he still felt guilty about how he had been with Lucas. And he figured maybe this could be a kind of penance or something. So he sat next to her and helped her shield the match's flame with his hands so she could light this beat-up looking cigarette butt.

"Oh shit!" she said. "It's fucking menthol. That's fancy."

She passed it to him.

Rick took a drag. It made him cough and become lightheaded. He passed it back.

"I saw what you did to the creeper?" she said.

"Who's the creeper?"

"That tall kid with the old lady sunglasses."

"His name's Lucas. He's actually really cool. Just a little too into sex."

"Whatever. It was intense how you just took him out like that. I like watching fights."

"It wasn't really a fight."

"Whatever."

They heard the groan of a screen door. The owner of the deli came out and told them to move on.

"We have a right to be here," Nicole said.

"No you don't. This is my deli. Move on. You are scaring away my customers."

"Fuck you," she said.

She stood up and reached for Rick's hand. He took it and stood with her.

They headed down the street. As they walked, her soggy shirtsleeve touched his hand and it was gross but also felt intimate.

They walked and gossiped and bitched about their teachers.

"I need a break," Nicole said. "I feel like my legs are about to give out."

They hadn't been walking long. Maybe half a mile or so. But he agreed to take a break. There was an old church nearby. He sat on front steps that were long and wide. She sat on his lap.

"Am I too extra-large for you?" she asked.

"No, I'm just small."

"I like small guys."

FOUR

AT FIRST HE felt embarrassed walking around with this crusty girl holding hands and stuff. She talked so loudly and cursed constantly. But none of the adults seemed to notice.

They walked around until their feet hurt then they cuddled on a bench.

"So I gotta be honest with you," she said. "I'm cool with us going steady but don't try to put your dick in me 'cause I'm not into babies. I think they are fucking gross."

He was shocked and overwhelmed.

This was a lot to process. He had never really crushed on a girl. Not the way Lucas liked to crush. But having a girlfriend sounded strange and fun and kinda cool. And he liked the idea of not having babies.

So he nodded his approval.

"I'll see you in school tomorrow."

"Are you leaving?"

"I gotta start walking home."

"Okay."

She walked away without kissing him.

Which he didn't mind. He was so much shorter than her. He didn't want to figure out that dynamic while they were standing.

FIVE

RICK SPENT MOST of that night worrying. He wanted to call Nicole and confirm they were really boyfriend and girlfriend. He just wanted to call and make sure.

Play it cool, he kept telling himself.

He couldn't understand why he was getting so worked up. Earlier that day, he had thought Nicole was a gross stoner.

Things felt too random. It was all just too sudden and strange. Maybe that was the problem.

The next day they passed each other on their way to class. But Nicole didn't seem to notice him. Things were hectic in the hallways though. And he was tiny. Way too tiny. Maybe she just didn't see him or something.

SIX

AT LUNCH, RICK sat on the bleachers in the gym and watched Nicole goofing around with her friends. Her friends looked grimy. But not as grimy as her.

She was still ignoring him. Part of him was relieved. The night before seemed so hidden and so private it barely felt like it existed. Now they were in a gym packed full of teenagers. It was hard to imagine being with her with so many people around.

He was about to join his friends in a game of HORSE when he saw Nicole approaching him.

"What up?" he said.

She gave him a hateful look, stuck her tongue out at him, and sat on his lap.

People were staring at them and talking about them. His buddy Lucas was all the way on the other side of the gym and even though he was wearing those sunglasses Rick could still tell he was staring. Rick felt very self-conscious.

"Well, hello!" Rick said.

"Shut up," she said.

"How was your day?"

"Can I ask you something important?" she said.

"Go for it."

"Do you believe in the female orgasm?"

"Sure."

"That's good. By the way, my parents want to meet you."

"You serious? When?"

"Tomorrow night. They want you to come over for dinner. You can come over at eight."

"Sure," he said. "I can do that."

She started chewing on the sleeve of her button down.

Rick liked her messy blond hair. It smelled like shampoo and cigarettes.

SEVEN

BEFORE HEADING OVER to Nicole's, Rick made sure to shower, masturbate, and shower again.

Around six, his mom offered him dinner. But he reminded her of his date.

"I'm very proud of you," she said.

"Mom, stop. You're making me seem like a reject. You are talking about me like it's weird that I have a girlfriend."

"Well, you are a bit of a late bloomer."

"I have pubes. I've had pubes for years."

"I'm just saying . . ."

"Are you talking about my Lego castle? Mom, I built that years ago."

"That was not years ago. That was a couple months ago at most."

"Mom, you have the worst memory. Sometimes I think you have dementia or something."

"Fuck off, I'm not that old."

"You smell old," Rick said.

He couldn't help but smile a little.

Then his mom grabbed him and pulled him close. She hugged

157

him and wrestled him and kissed the top of his head.

"Mom, stop," he said.

"I can't. I just love kissing your zitty forehead too much. I'm addicted."

"My head's not zitty."

They both laughed and continued wrestling.

EIGHT

NICOLE LIVED REALLY far away. Rick had never been in that section of town before. Everything was run down. At one point he thought he saw a mountain. But they lived on Long Island. It was big but there were no mountains.

"This is a weird place," his mom said. "Reminds me of upstate New York."

Nicole's house stood at the end of a long dirt driveway. Unlike the other homes in the area, her home looked new.

"Nice place," his mother said as they pulled into the driveway. "What do her parents do for a living?"

"How should I know?"

"Do you want me to come in and introduce myself?"

"No. I'll be fine."

He got out of the jeep and waved goodbye. Then he walked up to the house slowly, waiting for his mother to pull away. As soon as she was gone, he knocked on the door.

A younger man answered the door. He was lean and muscular and he was not wearing a shirt.

"Is Nicole here?" Rick asked.

The man felt his chest.

"You must be Rick? Are you the boy who got my sister pregnant?"

"What?"

"I'm just playing around with you."

Rick laughed in a way that made him a bit lightheaded.

The man shook his head.

"Damn, she likes them tiny. How old are you? Four?"

"I'm fourteen."

"Oh. Well, I guess that's a good thing. I was worried that my sister had turned into a pedophile. I mean, shit, I would love her and support her decisions no matter what. But life is complicated for a pedophile. Or so I've heard. I wouldn't know. I fuck women that are my age. The women I date have to be my age exactly, actually. I prefer them to even have the same birthday as me. That's rare though. But the closer they get to be my exact age, the sexier they look to me. Isn't that weird?"

Rick didn't know how to respond. He didn't want to offend this guy. He didn't want to seem too nervous either. Though, at this point, he knew it was probably too late for that.

"Danny, who's at the door?" he heard a woman's voice call out.

"It's Nicole's boyfriend."

"Invite him in."

Danny put his arms around Rick and led him inside. The house looked so sterile. Not new. But like it had been cleaned every day for many years. He walked Rick into the kitchen where Nicole's parents were busy working on dinner.

"These are my parents, Daren and Karen," Dan said. "They make me dinner sometimes."

"Nice to meet you," her father said.

He was a tall man with a well-kept mustache and broad shoulders. His skin was rough and he had small scars on his face. But he acted gentle. He had an easy smile and wore a baby blue polo shirt and shorts that showed off his powerful thighs.

"Can I get you anything?" Karen asked.

Her mother was attractive and bony and dressed well. She drank wine out of a tall glass and acted loose and friendly.

"Do you have any soda?"

"So much soda," she said.

She opened the fridge and handed him a can of soda. Rick opened the can and took a sip.

"Best soda I've ever had," he said.

Rick couldn't tell if he was being charming or nervous or both. Luckily her family started laughing.

NINE

THEY STOOD IN the kitchen and talked. Rick drank his soda and asked for another. Then he drank that soda and burped. Nobody laughed. They didn't seem disgusted or annoyed but they most certainly were not amused. Rick asked if he could get a third soda, but Nicole's mother said they were out. He knew this wasn't true. There were so many sodas in the refrigerator. He had seen them. They had sodas. They had so many sodas. They just didn't want to give him any.

"So where's Nicole?" Rick asked.

"Don't know," her dad said.

"Maybe she ran away again," Dan said.

"Nicole hasn't run away since she was little. Stop trying to scare little Ricky. And put a shirt on for Christ's sake."

Dan walked off and came back moments later with a lime green polo on.

"Maybe she's with her boyfriend," Dan said.

"This is her boyfriend," her mother said.

"Didn't she say she was getting us milk," her father said.

"I don't know," her mother said. "Wherever she is, I'm sure she will be back soon. Until then, we all go to the living room and get to know each other a bit better."

TEN

THE COUCH CUSHIONS were so soft. It almost felt inappropriate. He considered that he might be too small to sit on such deep, soft cushions.

"So tell us about yourself," Karen said.

"What do you want to know?"

"Ever killed a man?" Dan asked.

"No," Rick said.

"I was just kidding, buddy. Relax."

"I know."

"So you go to high school with my daughter?"

Rick nodded.

"Dude," Dan said, "do you have Mr. Stranford for math?"

"I have him for sequential two."

"Does his breath still smell like diapers?"

"It's gone way past the diaper smell and reached a whole new level," Rick said.

Dan laughed.

"Poor Mr. Stranford," Karen said. "I gave him homemade toothpaste every year for Christmas. It did no good though."

"How do you make homemade toothpaste?" Rick asked.

"It's simple," Karen said. "You use normal store bought

toothpaste first. Then after you are done brushing your teeth with like Colgate or something like that, you spit it up into a cup. We all collected our toothpaste spittle for about a week or so and, presto, we have homemade toothpaste."

This didn't seem legit to Rick, but he smiled at Nicole's mom as if he was impressed. Besides, she had a kind of beauty to her that made everything seem reasonable.

"Mom, didn't you date Mr. Stranford once back when you were little."

"For one thing," she said, "I was never little. I went through puberty when I was five. So by the time I met Sammy Stranford, I was pretty much a fully developed woman. I was a bit pudgy back then, but that was fun for boys. Sammy and I had health class together. We both got turned on by all the diagrams of male parts and female parts. Things were different back then. Those were simpler, saner times, you have to understand."

"Tell us about his breath," Dan said.

"Well, it smelled. That's for sure. But I have to admit, I kinda liked it. His breath smelled like arm pits and I have to admit, I liked that. All women secretly like the smell of dirty arm pits. Don't let them tell you any different, boys."

Rick smelled his own pits, which had a tangy peppermint odor to them. He had put on way too much deodorant and he regretted it.

She asked Rick some about his life. About his mother and his interests and stuff like that. Rick could tell he was boring her. She kept nodding off. But every time he stopped talking, she would ask another question.

"Hey, Mom," Dan said. "I think our show's on."

"*Goon Date*? Turn it on."

"What's *Goon Date*?" Rick asked.

"It's a dating show where ugly people go on dates together. It's a riot."

"You and my sister should be on this," Dan said.

"Be nice," Karen said.

"Do you know when Nicole will be back?" Rick asked.

Nicole's mother shrugged her shoulders.

ELEVEN

BY THE END of the hour-long television program, Karen had finished a few glasses of wine and fallen asleep.

Dan was still awake though. He was very awake. He was staring at Rick and hadn't blinked much.

"So you wanna smoke some crack?" Dan asked.

"What?" Rick said.

"You heard me."

"I don't know," Rick said. "I heard it's pretty bad for you."

"Not really. Not if you only do it once," Dan said.

"What does it do?"

"It gets you high. It makes you feel good. Are you retarded?"

"I mean, is it like weed?"

"No. Nothing like weed. It's better. It's way better."

Rick could still hear Nicole's father in the kitchen.

"Maybe another time," he said.

"Don't you trust me? Do you think we would make you do something that would hurt you in some way?"

"No, it's not that. It's just. I don't know. Crack is kinda intense."

"How would you know? You've never done it."

"I guess you have a point."

"So you are going to give it a try?"

"I guess so."

Dan started laughing wildly.

"You are fucked up, man!" he said. "I can't believe you were about to do crack. That's so messed up. Who even does crack? Does my sister know she is dating a crackhead?"

"What? No. I mean, I'm not a crackhead. I thought you said it was no big deal."

"I never said that. Holy shit. My sister is dating a crack fiend."

TWELVE

ANOTHER EPISODE OF *Goon Date* came on. Rick watched the TV intently. He was trying to act calm and unaffected. He didn't want Dan to know he got to him. But eventually he snapped.

"Hey, Dan," Rick said.

"What do you want, cracky?"

"Don't tell Nicole about this."

"About what?"

"About how I was going to try crack."

"Why not? Are you the type of guy that has lots of secrets?"

"No."

"Then why do you care if we tell her you're a crack fiend?"

"Because I'm not."

Dan pretended to nod off. Then he scratched his crotch. Then he continued watching TV.

"Do you think she will care?" Rick asked.

"Care about what?"

"About me trying crack?"

"I don't know. I think you should be honest with her though," Dan said. "Honesty is key."

THIRTEEN

DAN TOOK HIS shirt off and fell asleep.

It was ten-thirty. Dinner hadn't started yet.

Rick wanted to see Nicole. He wanted to smell her hair. Where was she?

It was getting so late.

She could be off studying with a friend or something. Though she didn't seem like the type of girl that studied.

Rick stood and walked to the kitchen where he found Nicole's father standing over the stove.

"Cooking's hard," the man said.

Rick nodded.

"You cook?"

"No," Rick said. "I mean, I make cereal sometimes."

"I make things with my oven," Daren said.

"Are you worried about Nicole," Rick asked.

"No. Why would I be?"

"Because she's not here."

"So, she has her own life."

"But she invited me to come over tonight. And now she's not here. Don't you think that's a little strange?"

"It's important to not be so possessive," the father said.

FOURTEEN

DAREN OPENED THE oven.

"Fuck," he said.

"What's wrong?"

"There's nothing in here."

"What do you mean?"

"There's nothing in the oven. There's supposed to be something in the oven."

"You serious?"

"There needs to be something in there," Daren said. "Otherwise nothing will cook. And we will have nothing to eat."

"What were you planning on making?" Rick asked.

"I have to go find something to put in the oven," he said. "I gotta go."

"Go where?"

"I have to go get something to put in the oven."

"Like a grocery store?"

"I don't know."

"You should probably go to a grocery store."

"Don't tell my wife. Promise me you won't tell my wife."

"Sure."

"Swear to fucking God you won't tell my wife."

"I swear. I promise. I won't tell anybody."

FIFTEEN

THE HOUSE WAS quiet. Rick didn't know what to do with himself. He thought about calling home. Home seemed nice and comfortable. More comfortable than it had ever seemed before. He imagined it filled with dusty morning sunlight. He imagined every piece of furniture feeling as soft and warm as his mother's nightgown.

Rick walked over to the living room. Nicole's mother and her son were still asleep.

Rick found himself another soda in the refrigerator and started to drink it. He belched then the phone started to ring.

SIXTEEN

"HELLO?"

It was Nicole.

"Hello! Someone please pick up."

"Hello," Rick said.

"Rick, is that you?"

"Nicole, where the hell are you?"

"I'm in the shed."

"What?"

"I was taking a nap. Somebody locked me in. It was probably my shithead brother."

"What shed?"

"The fucking shed in my fucking backyard, stupid."

Rick looked out the window. He couldn't see anything but darkness.

"How long have you been in there?"

"I don't know. A while. Can you please come and get me out of here."

"Sure."

He hung up the phone then slid open the large glass door that led to the back deck.

There was nothing but darkness. It didn't feel like he was outside at all. It reminded him of the darkness of a basement or the cluttered closet he had liked hiding out in when he was a child.

He walked to the edge of the deck, felt the damp wooden railing, and followed it to a series of steps. Wind blew through trees in the distance. He headed in that direction, though he couldn't see any shed. It was dark. Dark like a closet or a basement or a movie theater or napping in church.

At one point, he looked back and saw the lights from the house. It seemed so far away now. How large was their property? He felt like he had been walking for a while. But he had also been walking slowly.

Finally he saw a shape and a sliver of light. As he got closer he could see the shed more clearly. It was green and almost looked like a little house. There were flowers planted around its perimeter.

"Nicole," he said.

He was speaking too quietly though. There was no way for her to hear him.

He walked up to the shed. A plank of wood crossing the two door handles was keeping the doors shut. Rick removed the wood and opened the door and winced at the bright light coming from the shed's opening.

"About time," Nicole said.

SEVENTEEN

NICOLE PUNCHED HIM in the shoulder.

"You saved my ass. I've been locked in that bullshit shed for so fucking long."

This seemed way too friendly of a hello. He wanted passion. He wanted groping affection. He did not want to be called buddy and then to get punched the way Lucas punched him on the shoulder.

"You look nice," he said.

"Stop being a dork," she said.

She punched him in the arm again.

"Don't punch me," Rick said. "That's domestic abuse."

"Oh, is it?" she said.

"Legally, yes."

She laughed.

"How long you been in there?" he asked.

"Most of the fucking day," she said.

"That sucks."

"My brother's a dick."

"I know. I met him."

"Did he molest you? Did he finger bang you?"

"No. At least I don't think so."

She laughed and hugged him. Her arms were long and warm.

"Touch my butt," she said. "I think my butt has hypothermia. It needs to be warmed up."

EIGHTEEN

AFTER HUGGING AND some butt touching, they climbed on top of the shed. They sat there and split a cigarette, which made Rick lightheaded.

He lay back and looked up at the pine trees. His eyes had adjusted to the darkness and he felt comfortable out there.

"The shed isn't so bad," Nicole said. "I could live in a place like that. I don't like being locked in there with no food. But if it wasn't locked and there was some food and shit, I could get into living there. Would you ever live in a shed?"

"No. I like houses too much."

"Houses are ruining the planet," she said. "With their fucking air conditioners and shit."

As they bickered, a cool breeze passed over them. They both stayed still and breathed it in, loving the way pine tasted on the air.

NINETEEN

"I **HAVE TO** tell you a secret," Rick said.

"Well go on."

"I told your brother I'd smoke crack."

"Why did you do that?"

"I don't know."

She laughed and lay back and put her head against his.

He put his hand on her belly.

"Oh, you're a toucher. I didn't know that."

"Is it bad?" he asked.

She didn't respond.

He kept his hand on her belly.

"Do you mind that I have some belly hair?" she asked.

"No."

He sounded so serious. He didn't want to sound so goddamn serious. But he couldn't help it.

"I feel like I might be turning into an ape creature."

"Shut up," he said. "You have nice belly skin."

"I'm serious. I caught my brother praying one night. He was standing over my bed praying that I become an ape creature."

TWENTY

SOMEONE WAS IN the woods. Someone was calling Rick's name.

"What the fuck is that?"

"Probably just a ghost," Nicole said. "It's probably just a puberty ghost."

"What the fuck is that?"

"It's what your jizz is made out of."

"That's stupid."

"Is not. Puberty ghosts hide in your balls. Then they come out during sex and haunt the belly of females until they have flesh again."

"It's kinda a cool idea."

He heard it again. It was calling for him.

"I think that's Lucas," Rick said.

"Who?"

"My buddy, Lucas."

"What is he doing here?"

"Don't know. I think he's been spying on us."

"That's kinda sexy."

"It is?"

"Sure."

"What should we do?"

"Go talk to him. He obviously wants to talk to you."

"You wanna come with?"

"Are you scared he's going to get revenge on you?"

"I don't know."

"I don't want to deal with all that revenge shit. I'm staying here."

TWENTY-ONE

RICK FOLLOWED HIS friend's voice. He kept looking back to make sure he could see the light coming from the shed. There was an open patch where things seemed less dark. His friend sat on a large rock.

"Rick," he said. "How you doing?"

"Good, man. What are you doing here?"

"I needed to see you."

Lucas stood up and approached his friend. He felt confused. What was his friend doing out here so late at night? He wanted to hit him and tell him to stop being so fucking weird and sensitive and creepy all the time.

Instead, they embraced. And Rick became overwhelmed with affection. He appreciated how familiar his friend felt.

"I'm sorry," Rick said. "I'm sorry I hit you with the basketball. I'm sorry I'm always so annoyed with you. I'm sorry I'm dating the girl you liked."

"It's okay, man. It's really okay."

"I'm such a shitty friend," Rick said.

"No, you're the best. I love you, Rick."

"I love you too, man."

"You are the best man I have ever known."

"Thanks."

"You are an inspiration."

"Cool, you too."

"So, you're in a relationship now?"

"I guess so."

"Is it nice?"

"She's warm," Rick said.

"I bet," Lucas said. "Can I feel your cock?"

"Sure."

Lucas reached into Rick's shorts. He grabbed his friend's erection.

"It's gotten bigger," Lucas said.

"It has?"

"You have relationship cock now. Relationship cocks are bigger than normal cocks."

TWENTY-TWO

RICK CLIMBED BACK on top of the shed.

Nicole smoked. Then blew cigarette smoke up at the night sky.

"How's Lucas?" she asked.

"He's good. He gave me his sunglasses."

"I noticed. They actually look kinda cool on you."

"They make things look really different."

"How so?"

"Well, for one thing, I can barely see anything."

Nicole laughed so hard Rick felt like she was going to wake the whole world up.

He took his glasses off.

Nicole lay on her back and smiled at him and put her arms behind her head.

"Can I see your breasts?" he asked.

"Maybe. You have to see for yourself. I might let you. I might break all your fingers."

Rick pulled her shirt up. She wasn't wearing a bra. Her breasts were large and covered in stretch marks. Even in the dark he could see how red they were. They looked like streams of lava.

He touched them. And sucked on them.

She tasted sweaty.

TWENTY-THREE

"WAS THAT THE first boob you ever sucked on?"

"No. Lucas paid me five bucks to suck on Kevin Semore's man boob once."

"But my boob was the first fully female boob you ever sucked on?"

"Yes. It was."

"I hope it was memorable."

TWENTY-FOUR

RICK AND NICOLE got off the shed and walked around. They occasionally made faces at each other. At one point Nicole made sex sounds or at least what Rick assumed were sex sounds. Then, right as she was getting to the climax, she made a long, bubbly fart sound. They laughed and continued wandering around.

They made their way to the house and saw Nicole's family was sitting around the dining room table eating pizza. Nicole didn't want to go inside. She was still mad about being locked in the shed. Rick was hungry, but he wanted to stay outside with Nicole.

"My dad made pizza," she said. "He's really good at making pizza."

"I think he bought it."

"I know. That's why it's so good."

"I guess."

"Do you think my mom's pretty?" she asked.

"Yeah, but not in the same way that you're pretty."

"I think your mom's pretty. I think she's really beautiful."

"My mom's fat."

"So what?"

"She has chipmunk face."

"I've seen your mom pick you up from school. She's really sweet and has really nice eyes. She's beautiful. What's wrong with you?"

"Were you spying on me?"

Rick tried to sound flirtatious. But Nicole didn't seem amused.

"I'm being serious, you shithead. Your mom's pretty."

"Sorry, I don't want to fuck my mom."

"I never said anything about fucking."

"Sorry, I don't want to dry hump my mom."

"I never said anything about dry humping either."

"Then what are you talking about?"

"Just looking nice, I guess."

TWENTY-FIVE

THEY WALKED INTO the woods. Occasionally they saw lights from other houses. Or maybe it was Nicole's place. Rick couldn't tell. It was very disorienting. Nicole seemed to know where she was going though. He held her hand and held onto it. Their hands became sweaty. It reminded him of the time his mother had taken him to New York City to see *Cats* on Broadway.

"I'm thinking of joining the army," Nicole said. "Rick, would you run away and join the army with me?"

"I feel like this is a trick question."

"Are you afraid of battle?"

"I don't want to be shot to death."

"Don't you want to have strong survival skills?"

"I think there are other ways to figure this out that would involve less going to war."

"Fuck it, the military would probably be boring as shit anyway."

TWENTY-SIX

THEY HEADED BACK to the shed and climbed onto the roof and cuddled and molested each other some more. Then they got bored of that. Well, Nicole got bored. They walked back to her house. Dinner was over.

The back door was locked.

They walked around front but that door was locked, as well.

"Those fuckwads," Nicole said.

"Is there any other way in?"

"I'm sure it's all locked."

"We could check."

"No. Let's just break a window."

She karate kicked the window near the entrance. It shattered.

"Holy shit!" Rick yelled. "Are you okay?"

Nicole laughed hard and breathlessly.

"I've never done that before," she said.

"Are you bleeding?"

"No, I don't think so."

She pulled her jeans down. Her legs looked pale in the moon-light.

"Can you check to make sure I don't have too many wounds?"

Rick kneeled and inspected her legs. His hands shook as he felt her leg for wounds. There were lots of little hairs on her lower calf but her upper legs, the thigh or whatever they call it, felt nice and smooth.

Her underpants were baggy, what his buddies called granny panties.

"I think you're okay."

"No shit?"

"I can't find a single cut."

"Fuck yeah. I should do this for a living. I could be a robber. A cat burglar or some shit."

"I think it was just beginner's luck."

She had Rick crawl through the window and unlock the door.

Rick followed her through the house. The lights were off and she did not want to turn them back on.

She found her mother's purse on the kitchen table, reached in, and found her mace.

"What is that?" Rick asked her.

"It's like a magic potion," she told him.

"What are we going to do with it?"

"Play a prank on my family."

Rick smiled.

"I love pranks."

TWENTY-SEVEN

THEY HEADED TO her parents' room. The hallways were so dark it was hard to breathe.

"Is this like a thing you guys do?" Rick asked.

"What is a thing?"

"This whole pranking thing. Do you guys prank each other a lot?"

"No."

Her parents lay in bed sleeping naked. The blankets barely covered their bodies. Rick could see Daren's formidable penis and his wife's muscular back and flat but still elegant buttocks.

"MOM! DAD!" Nicole yelled. "WAKE UP!"

Her dad opened his eyes.

"What's going on? Damn it, Nicky, you know I need my rest. What the fuck is the matter with you?"

Nicole reached her arm out, aiming the canister at her father's eyes. She pushed down and there was a soft, wet sound.

Her father screamed. It was really loud and high pitched, like a child's. He flailed around until he fell off the bed. Then he started flopping around like a fish.

Her mother woke up next.

"What the hell?" she said.

She sounded more annoyed than scared.

Nicole aimed the mace at her and sprayed.

For a moment her mother seemed immune. Then she put her hands over her eyes like she was trying to extinguish the fire. This didn't work. Soon she started screaming. It was so loud. Rick felt nauseous.

Now both parents were in hysterics. Rick had no idea mace hurt so badly. Her father had wet himself. Her mother was punching her eyes over and over.

Her brother came into the room.

"Mom, Dad, what's going on?" his voice sounded pitiful. Rick hated it. He hated it so much.

Nicole sprayed her brother with the mace. He fell to his knees, moaning, and howled.

Maybe they were allergic or something, Rick thought. Maybe this is an extra potent can of mace.

There were so many nauseating sounds going on at once. Rick could barely stand it.

Finally, Nicole's mother gained some composure. She looked at them with swollen, moist and red eyes.

"NICKY!"

TWENTY-EIGHT

NICOLE AND RICK ran out of the house, across the dewy lawn and into the woods on the other side of the street.

As soon as they were in the woods, they felt safe. They hid behind a large oak and watched Nicole's family stumble out of the house.

The porch light was bright and lit most of the front yard. Nicole's family moaned and screamed and fell and wandered blindly. They called out to their daughter. They were angry, sure. But they also seemed deeply concerned and the combination made Rick feel uneasy. He had trouble breathing.

"What should we do?" Rick said.

"I don't know. I had no idea mace hurt this badly. Do you think they will be blind forever?"

"I don't know."

"Oh God!" Nicole said. "What have I done?"

Nicole had the mace pointed the wrong way.

"I really fucked up this time," she said.

"I'm sure everything will be okay," he said.

But his voice was flimsy and cheap and unconvincing.

Nicole looked at the mace. She pointed it toward herself.

"What are you doing?" Rick asked.

"I don't know."

She sprayed the mace in her own eye and screamed. Her scream sounded like her mother's. It was almost elegant. But it didn't last long.

The scream turned into a growl and she fell to her knees and struck the ground with her fists.

"Fuck. Fuck. Oh Jesus fucking Christ!" she said. "It really fucking hurts! I didn't realize it hurt this much! Oh fuck!"

She puked a bit.

Then almost screamed again.

TWENTY-NINE

RICK FELT HELPLESS as he led his girlfriend through the woods. She was stumbling and falling a lot and she was way bigger than him and in a lot of pain and, to top things off, he had no idea where he was.

"Hey, Nicole, do you have any idea where we are?"

"My fucking eyes still hurt! Why won't the pain stop?" she yelled.

He kept moving.

THIRTY

FOR A MILE or so Nicole had started cursing God and spraying the mace around. To protect his eyes, Rick put on his friend's sunglasses.

This made it near impossible to see at first. But then he noticed a trail. It looked like a long dark rug was on the ground. But . . .

When he took his glasses off, Rick couldn't see anything. No trail. Nothing.

He put them back on. For a moment. More nothing.

Then he started to see the trail again.

He grabbed Nicole's hand and dragged her through her woods, praying he wouldn't walk into anything.

THIRTY-ONE

A NICE BREEZE worked its way through the forest. It smelled sweet and manly. Rick led them toward the smell. Soon they came into a clearing. They walked through tall reeds. Waves crashed in the distance. They rushed toward it. Nicole was leading them now.

Soon they were sliding down a tall dune and making their way to the water. Rick couldn't understand how they had gotten to the ocean. They had been walking for a long time. But not that long. He couldn't recognize the beach at all. This was not Sagmaine Beach. He couldn't see any beach houses or a lifeguard stand. This beach looked kinda abandoned. Not that a beach can look any other way at night.

Nicole rushed to the water and dove in. He thought about joining her. But the waves were large and he couldn't see her and the water he had stepped into was so cold it hurt his bones.

He watched Nicole swim and thought she looked beautiful. Waves crashed and foamy water rushed up to him. Rick backed away.

He couldn't see Nicole. There were waves and foam and more waves.

She's probably fine, he kept telling himself. Don't act all scared and dorky and shit. But he couldn't shake the panic.

He took his glasses off so he could see better.

THIRTY-TWO

NOW THE OCEAN seemed calm. The waves were small. The moon was bright and reflected off the small waves. It wasn't so dark now. But he still couldn't see Nicole.

He was about to start crying, so he put the glasses back on.

THIRTY-THREE

NICOLE STUMBLED OUT of the water, laughing.

"That felt so good. My eyes feel so much better now."

She ran up to Rick and hugged him.

"You're so wet and cold," he said.

THIRTY-FOUR

THEY CUDDLED ON the beach together. Rick was soaked. He felt like his clothing had absorbed all the water off Nicole. He was freezing. But enjoyed cuddling and feeling her belly.

"We should dig a hole," Nicole said. "And live in the hole, then get roommates and charge them rent."

"What about high tide? The hole would fill up with water."

"We'll probably need scuba gear."

They kissed. She tasted salty and cold.

THIRTY-FIVE

A MAN STUMBLED onto the beach and into the ocean. Rick didn't tell Nicole what he had seen. He didn't want to ruin the moment. But then he saw the shadow of a shark. Then he saw glowing green eyes. Then he heard screaming and the water filled with blood. At first the blood was bright. Then its color dimmed.

THIRTY-SIX

"I THINK THAT was your dad," Rick said.

"No, I doubt it."

"Nicole, I am pretty sure that was your dad. He looked like your dad."

"It's dark. I could barely see the dude. I think it was just some rich guy."

"That shark ate him."

"I didn't see any shark."

"Are you sure?"

She didn't respond.

Rick was afraid her brother and her mother would stumble into the ocean and get eaten, as well. But he kept that to himself.

The shark was still swimming in the waves. It was big. Its eyes were really, really green.

Rick was not able to relax until the shark finally swam out of sight.

THIRTY-SEVEN

NICOLE GATHERED UP some driftwood and they managed to get a fire going. That warmed them up a bit. Rick loved the way she looked in the firelight. He took his wet shirt off and placed it near the fire to dry it off.

"Look at your little nipples," Nicole said.

Rick laughed.

Nicole smiled, then stood up and started dancing around the fire like she was a ballerina that had smoked way too much weed or like the clouds overhead that were low and swirled and looked purple and red. Maybe his glasses made the sky look that way. He wasn't sure. He didn't want to take them off and find out what things really looked like.

FAMILY-SIZED

GWEN SAW TWO beached whales and became so excited she started jumping up and down.

"Mom? Dad?" she called out to them.

The whales looked at her.

"You've come back for me!" she yelled.

She ran up to them.

She tried to hug them but they were too big. Her human arms couldn't reach around their big fat whale bodies.

"I always knew you would come back," she kept saying.

She told them about her life. It was a long story. There were lots of boring parts.

"I'm just so glad you are here," she said.

She tried to hug them again. They were still too big. Her arms were still too human.

It was a hot day. Her parents looked thirsty.

"Don't worry," she said. "I'll get you some water."

She walked back to the parking lot and got in her Saab and headed toward Easthampton.

"WHERE THE FUCK CAN I BUY WATER?" she screamed.

The movie theater had just opened. They sold lots of stuff there. They had hot dogs and soda and popcorn and all sorts of candy. She decided to get them Diet Pepsi. Diet Pepsi was healthier and her parents were fat. Way too fat.

But, in order to get inside she had to buy a movie ticket.

She bought a ticket to *Rocky XXII.*

At first she had no actual interest in watching the movie. She just wanted access to buy some diet soda for her parents. But the idea of buying a movie ticket and not seeing the movie felt wasteful to her. So she watched the movie.

It was really good. Rocky had a bunch of grandkids and yelled at them a lot. He told them about discipline and perseverance and, for some reason, watching this made Gwen really emotional. She cried a little.

Then she thought about her parents and how much she missed them and cried some more.

After the movie she bought as much diet soda as she could carry.

She put the sodas in the trunk of her car and started driving toward the beach.

The beach felt really far away.

And driving was just so hard sometimes.

By the time she finally got there, it was night.

She gathered up all the sodas from her trunk and headed to the beach.

"MOM! DAD! I BOUGHT YOU DIET SODA!" she yelled.

The two whales smelled strange and didn't breathe much.

She poured the sodas on them.

"Isn't it so good," she said.

It had been a long day.

After feeding her parents all that soda, Gwen decided to take a nap, using one of their fins as a blanket.

When she woke up she noticed they weren't breathing at all.

And they smelled really bad.

"Mom? Dad? Please wake up?"

She hurled her body on theirs.

She begged them to wake up.

And she cried.

She hit them and clawed at them and begged them to come back to life. But they didn't listen.

The sun was rising.

The waves were loud and comforting in all the wrong ways.

Justin Grimbol lives in Vermont. He works as a Home Health Aide and buys books then sells books and he also writes books and tries to sell those too. He does not make much money. He's kind of a chump. A dead beat. A mooch. But he has written some books. And this is his first collection of short stories.

Other **Atlatl Press** Books

Elaine by Ben Arzate
Bird Castles by Justin Grimbol
Fuck Happiness by Kirk Jones
Impossible Driveways by Justin Grimbol
Giraffe Carcass by J. Peter W.
Shining the Light by A.S. Coomer
Failure As a Way of Life by Andersen Prunty
Hold for Release Until the End of the World
by C.V. Hunt
Die Empty by Kirk Jones
Mud Season by Justin Grimbol
Death Metal Epic (Book Two: Goat Song Sacrifice)
by Dean Swinford
Come Home, We Love You Still by Justin Grimbol
We Did Everything Wrong by C.V. Hunt
Squirm With Me by Andersen Prunty
Hard Bodies by Justin Grimbol
Arafat Mountain by Mike Kleine
Drinking Until Morning by Justin Grimbol
Thanks For Ruining My Life by C.V. Hunt
Death Metal Epic (Book One: The Inverted Katabasis)
by Dean Swinford
Fill the Grand Canyon and Live Forever by Andersen Prunty
Mastodon Farm by Mike Kleine
Fuckness by Andersen Prunty
Losing the Light by Brian Cartwright
They Had Goat Heads by D. Harlan Wilson
The Beard by Andersen Prunty